Freak Party

Freak Party, Volume 1

Aiden Rivers

Published by Century Books, 2024.

This is a work of fiction. Similarities to real people, places, or events are entirely coincidental.

FREAK PARTY

First edition. November 5, 2024.

Copyright © 2024 Aiden Rivers.

ISBN: 979-8227671936

Written by Aiden Rivers.

Also by Aiden Rivers

Christmas Thriller
Christmas Eve Revenge
Christmas Lights
The Silent Night Curse

Freak Party
Freak Party
Freak Party: Shadows of Fame

Standalone
Crimes of Passion: The Silence Beneath
Echoes of Obsession
Island of Hearts
The Mirror's Edge
The Shadow Mind
Beyond the Goal: A Love Unwritten
Gay Short Stories
Hearts in the Outfield

Chapter 1: The Invitation

The invitation arrived on an otherwise typical Wednesday evening, tucked within a stack of bills and advertisements in Elliot's mailbox. His usual routine—dragging himself through a loop of uninspired work, barely scraping by, and dreaming of a breakthrough—was broken the moment he glimpsed the heavy, textured envelope emblazoned with a silver insignia: *W.D.*, the unmistakable initials of Winston Devereaux.

Elliot's pulse quickened. It wasn't a mistake, he assured himself. This was *the* invitation, the one he'd only heard of through whispered rumors at after-parties and in the dimly lit bars where hopefuls like him gathered to share stories of near-misses and dream gigs. An invitation to Winston's annual White Party wasn't just an event. It was an initiation—a golden ticket for emerging artists and ambitious professionals, and possibly, a life-altering experience.

As he opened the envelope, the first page was a meticulously designed invitation card in crisp, minimalist style. The bold, scripted font read:

"You're Invited to an Exclusive Evening with Winston Devereaux at The White Party"

The letters seemed to gleam under his apartment's dim lighting, as though challenging him to imagine the grandeur that awaited. He scanned through the elegant script, soaking in the fine details: the date, location, and strict dress code. The dress code was a classic *white-only attire*, reinforcing an air of exclusivity that made the White Party feel like a modern legend. There was a detailed map to the mansion—a sprawling estate perched along a private cliffside, known to locals as "Devereaux's Lair." The name had always sounded ominous, but right now, all Elliot could picture were its vast open spaces and the glittering city skyline.

He knew this was more than just a social event; it was his chance to prove himself. The list of people who had attended the White Party in the past was as long as it was illustrious. From international music icons and moguls to actors and billionaire entrepreneurs, every power player in the entertainment industry had been there. It was a space where deals were forged, collaborations took root, and fortunes shifted in a single evening.

Elliot's hands trembled as he put down the invitation. Winston Devereaux, for all his larger-than-life status, was a man shrouded in mystery. Known as a boundary-breaking mogul, he'd been behind countless pop culture phenomena, and his parties had a reputation—intense, extravagant, borderline surreal. Some spoke of the wild indulgences Winston offered his guests, while others hinted at undercurrents darker than what the media reported. But Elliot shook off those thoughts. After all, these were just rumors, probably stoked by jealousy from those left out.

The invitation glimmered like a promise. *This is my time,* he thought, looking around at his modest apartment, where remnants of his day job cluttered the corners, reminding him of all the days he'd spent chasing dead-end leads and empty promises. Here was his chance to finally be seen by someone who could change his career overnight.

FREAK PARTY

Elliot stood before his modest closet, fingers trailing over his limited collection of shirts and slacks. He felt the weight of the event looming over him, knowing that tonight would require more than just any outfit; it called for transformation. After scouring secondhand shops and spending what little he had, he finally found a crisp, fitted white suit. It was perfect—sophisticated, clean, and, he hoped, enough to make him look like he belonged.

As he tried on the suit, he caught his reflection in the mirror. The person staring back looked poised, confident—everything he'd spent years trying to become. He took a deep breath, as if filling his lungs with the courage he'd need for tonight.

For the next hour, he practiced introductions, imagining the influential people he might encounter. He rehearsed his name and his craft with the precision of someone walking a tightrope, a hint of self-doubt threading through each word. To distract himself, he conjured fantasies of meaningful conversations, of lingering eyes and knowing nods. He pictured Winston himself recognizing his potential, or perhaps a renowned artist leaning in and saying, "I want to work with you."

It was ambitious, even a little absurd, but Elliot clung to the dream. It was a buoy, a beacon of hope in an industry that rarely showed mercy. Tonight wasn't just a party—it was the start of the life he'd envisioned.

As he stepped into the entryway, Elliot was nearly overwhelmed by the scene unfolding before him. It was more than just a party; it was an orchestration of wealth, style, and allure that enveloped every guest who passed through the grand doors. The mansion's open-air foyer led into a marble hallway illuminated by ornate crystal chandeliers, their flickering lights

AIDEN RIVERS

casting golden shadows that only intensified the mansion's mystique. The high ceilings seemed to disappear into infinity, drawing every eye upward before leading them into the heart of the gathering.

Elliot took a slow, deep breath, attempting to ground himself amidst the wave of luxury that surrounded him. Servers dressed in all-white suits circulated the floor, carrying trays adorned with champagne flutes that sparkled under the lights. The air was thick with the fragrance of high-end perfumes, exotic scents blending together in an intoxicating cloud that made the room feel like a living, breathing entity. Each corner of the vast space was meticulously designed for elegance, from the artfully arranged white roses on marble pedestals to the cascading silk drapes that framed the windows overlooking the gardens.

He was almost immediately aware of the sheer volume of influential figures present. Celebrities he had only seen on magazine covers or TV screens were milling around casually, chatting and laughing as though this kind of night was routine for them. The sight was thrilling and intimidating in equal measure. There, just a few feet away, was a legendary hip-hop artist known for his intense privacy; nearby, a famous model laughed with an A-list actor. He spotted a few high-profile music producers too—people who, in some distant way, might have an interest in his work.

For a moment, Elliot felt a pang of doubt. Was he truly ready for this? He'd been so focused on getting here, on scoring an invitation, that the actual experience of standing in the midst of it felt almost surreal. But he quickly dismissed his hesitation. This was his world now, at least for tonight. And he reminded

FREAK PARTY 5

himself that this was not just a party but a unique opportunity—a chance to mingle, to see, and most importantly, to be seen.

Summoning a bit of courage, he took a glass of champagne from a passing server and held it carefully, trying to blend in with the crowd. He reminded himself to keep his posture relaxed, adopting the easy confidence he had seen in music videos and interviews. After all, he was a rising music producer; tonight, he was not an outsider but a guest.

A few steps into the party, Elliot noticed an older gentleman who appeared to be sizing him up from across the room. The man's gaze lingered, cool and assessing, before he finally nodded with an approving look. That small, subtle nod ignited a spark of confidence within Elliot, a sign that maybe he did belong here after all.

As he moved deeper into the crowd, he felt the energy in the room shift slightly, like an undercurrent pulling him forward. Somewhere nearby, he overheard two guests whispering in low voices about a private section at the back of the mansion, reserved for only the "most trusted." The whispering, almost conspiratorial in tone, piqued his curiosity. He filed the information away, wondering if he might somehow gain access to this secretive space by the end of the night.

Just then, a familiar face caught his eye—an up-and-coming singer he'd once worked with at a small studio downtown. Their eyes met across the room, and she waved him over, her smile warm and welcoming. It was a small reassurance amid the overwhelming glamour, a reminder of his purpose and potential. She introduced him to a couple of her friends, each one more striking than the last, and he found himself relaxing slightly, easing into conversation as he absorbed the subtleties of the high-stakes environment around him.

With every passing moment, Elliot felt himself becoming part of the rhythm of the night. The initial wave of nerves had receded, replaced by a sense of anticipation. This world, vibrant and intense, was opening up before him, layer by layer, inviting him to step deeper into its secrets.

Chapter 2: First Impressions

As the evening unfolded, Elliot found himself enveloped in a whirlwind of laughter, chatter, and music that seemed to pulse in rhythm with the vibrant atmosphere of the party. He navigated through the crowd, feeling increasingly at ease among the elegantly dressed guests. The initial nerves that had gripped him at the entrance began to dissipate, replaced by a growing sense of belonging. Each encounter felt like a stepping stone, a connection that could lead him deeper into the world he had long aspired to join.

He approached a small group gathered around a grand piano, where a well-known singer was entertaining guests with a smooth rendition of a classic ballad. Elliot watched as the crowd swayed gently, their faces lit with delight, captivated by the performance. The singer's voice was rich and inviting, drawing everyone in as if they were part of a private concert. It was a stark contrast to the bright lights and energetic beats of the music industry he had come to know; this was an intimate display of talent that left Elliot in awe. The crowd's energy was infectious, and he couldn't help but smile, swaying slightly to the melody.

When the song ended, the singer stepped off the piano stool, graciously accepting compliments and applause from the audience. Elliot seized the moment, approaching her with genuine enthusiasm. "Your voice is incredible," he said, trying to match her relaxed demeanor. "I've heard you on the radio, but seeing you live is something else."

Her smile was radiant as she turned to him, her eyes sparkling with warmth. "Thank you! It's always great to connect with new faces. What do you do?" she asked, genuinely interested.

"I'm a music producer," he replied, feeling a mix of pride and vulnerability. "Just starting out, really. Trying to make a name for myself."

"Ah, the hustle!" she exclaimed, nodding knowingly. "It's tough, but the right connections can make all the difference. If you're good, you'll find your way. Just keep pushing."

Elliot appreciated her encouraging words, feeling a sense of camaraderie in the shared struggle of carving out a path in the industry. The conversation flowed effortlessly, and he found himself laughing and sharing anecdotes about his early days in the business, how he had practically lived at the local recording studio, dreaming of one day working with the stars.

As they spoke, he became aware of the connections forming around him. One of her friends, a stylish man with a flair for fashion, joined the conversation, introducing himself as a stylist known for working with some of the biggest names in the industry. The more they chatted, the more Elliot realized how intertwined their worlds were. This was no longer a simple gathering; it was a nexus of talent and ambition, all under the same roof.

Elliot felt a spark of inspiration as he moved from group to group, exchanging pleasantries and sharing ideas with different partygoers. He found himself speaking to a director who was scouting new talent for his upcoming project, and a writer whose recent screenplay had gained considerable acclaim. Each interaction seemed to reinforce the idea that this was a place where dreams could be ignited, where potential could be recognized in a mere conversation.

The casual elegance of the guests made the evening feel both glamorous and grounded. Elliot admired how effortlessly they navigated their status, treating one another as equals despite their differing levels of fame. He was enchanted by the genuine connections forming all around him, noting how easily they moved between discussions about their careers to light-hearted banter and shared laughter.

In those moments, Elliot realized that this was exactly what he had longed for—a chance to mingle among the influential, to see firsthand the informal exchanges that often led to powerful collaborations. The atmosphere thrummed with potential, and he felt more determined than ever to seize every opportunity that came his way.

As the night wore on, he took a moment to step back, scanning the room filled with ambition and creativity. Each conversation felt like a thread weaving him deeper into this intricate tapestry of the music industry. He knew he was at the threshold of something significant, a pivotal moment that could shape his future. He resolved to embrace it fully, confident that every interaction could be the one that propelled him into the spotlight he had always dreamed of.

As the evening progressed, Elliot's heart raced with anticipation. He knew the mogul, Victor Astor, was the man behind the event—the mastermind whose influence had shaped countless careers in the music industry. His reputation preceded him, painted as a larger-than-life figure whose keen instincts and charisma drew people in like moths to a flame. Elliot had heard the stories: how Victor could turn a struggling artist into a household name overnight, how he commanded respect and admiration from everyone in the room.

While mingling, Elliot caught a glimpse of Victor across the room. He stood tall, exuding an aura of confidence that was hard to ignore. His tailored suit, perfectly fitted, accentuated his commanding presence, and the way he effortlessly navigated through the crowd spoke of years spent mastering the art of influence. As Victor engaged in conversation, laughter and genuine warmth emanated from his interactions, drawing people closer as they vied for his attention.

Elliot watched, entranced, as Victor's magnetic personality seemed to light up the room. People leaned in to hear his words, hanging on every syllable, captivated by his storytelling. It was as if Victor had a spellbinding effect on those around him. In that moment, Elliot felt a blend of admiration and trepidation. This was the kind of man he aspired to be—a beacon of success, charisma, and creativity.

Just then, Victor's gaze met Elliot's, and for a brief moment, time seemed to stand still. A smile broke across Victor's face, warm and inviting, as he made his way toward Elliot. Elliot's breath caught in his throat; this was the moment he had been waiting for, an opportunity to introduce himself and make an impression. As Victor approached, the buzz of the party faded into the background, leaving only the two of them in focus.

"Hey there, I haven't seen you around before," Victor said, his voice smooth and confident, laced with a hint of curiosity. "I'm Victor Astor."

"Elliot," he replied, extending his hand, trying to keep his composure intact. "I'm a music producer, just starting out."

FREAK PARTY 11

Victor's grip was firm, and Elliot felt an electric spark as their hands connected. "Nice to meet you, Elliot. The fresh faces are always welcome here. What kind of music are you into?"

Elliot found himself momentarily tongue-tied, struck by the warmth of Victor's presence. "I work primarily in pop and indie music," he managed, mentally kicking himself for being so starstruck. "I love blending genres and finding new sounds."

"Sounds like you've got a good ear," Victor replied, his eyes glimmering with interest. "That's essential in this business. Keep experimenting; it's what separates the good from the great."

Encouraged by Victor's words, Elliot's confidence surged. "Thank you. I believe music should push boundaries. It's what inspires me."

Victor nodded, his expression thoughtful. "That's the spirit! Innovation is key. You never know who might be listening or what opportunity might come knocking."

Just then, the moment was interrupted by a group of people who flocked to Victor, eager to share their ideas and gain his insight. Elliot stepped back slightly, watching as Victor seamlessly transitioned from one conversation to another, his presence a magnetic force that commanded attention.

Even as the conversation shifted away, Elliot couldn't shake the feeling that he had glimpsed something extraordinary in Victor's charisma—an enigmatic energy that radiated confidence and inspiration. It left a lasting impression on him, igniting a fire within him to not only connect with Victor but to embody that same spirit of innovation and passion.

As the evening continued to unfold, Elliot felt a renewed sense of purpose. He was reminded that this world was one of possibilities, a place where dreams could be realized with the right connections and a sprinkle of luck. Meeting Victor Astor, even for a fleeting moment, had reinforced his belief in his aspirations and reminded him of the incredible journey that lay ahead.

As the evening unfolded, Elliot found himself wandering deeper into the opulence of the party, the atmosphere thick with glamour and ambition. The hum of laughter and lively conversations surrounded him, but his attention was drawn to a series of private VIP rooms tucked away from the main gathering. Each room had its own distinct aura, lavishly decorated and shielded by imposing security personnel who maintained a watchful eye over the entrances.

Curiosity flickered within Elliot. What was happening behind those closed doors? He could imagine the kind of conversations taking place—the whispers of deals being struck, collaborations being forged, and the elite of the industry discussing projects that could change the course of music history. His mind raced with possibilities, picturing the kind of talent that could be tucked away in those exclusive spaces, perhaps even Victor Astor himself.

Elliot's heart raced at the thought of stepping beyond those velvet ropes. He envisioned himself in one of those rooms, surrounded by artists and producers, sharing ideas and inspirations that could elevate his career. He yearned for a glimpse into that world, to understand the secrets of success that lay hidden just out of reach. The thought both thrilled and intimidated him.

With each passing moment, he became more entranced by the allure of the VIP sections. They were like siren calls, beckoning him to explore their depths. It wasn't just the

FREAK PARTY   13

exclusivity that fascinated him; it was the promise of what those spaces represented—success, influence, and the power to shape the music industry. He could picture himself standing in a room like that, pitching his ideas to the very people who could help him realize his dreams.

As he continued to observe the flow of the party, he noticed small clusters of people slipping in and out of the rooms, laughter spilling out and creating an inviting yet mysterious atmosphere. Some guests appeared more relaxed, their voices animated, while others had a more serious demeanor, engaged in what seemed to be intense discussions.

Elliot's gaze was particularly drawn to a couple of young producers he had seen earlier mingling at the bar. They had recently signed a major label deal, and their presence in one of the VIP rooms made his heart quicken with envy and desire. He wanted to be part of that circle, to forge connections with the artists and executives who could propel him forward.

He took a deep breath, weighing his options. Should he attempt to join the throngs of people slipping into those exclusive areas? He imagined himself approaching the security guard, flashing his best smile and the charming persona he had rehearsed in his head. But doubt crept in—what if he was turned away? What if they dismissed him as just another hopeful aspiring producer?

Despite the anxiety swirling in his stomach, the allure of the VIP rooms was undeniable. He could almost feel the energy radiating from within those walls, a promise of opportunity waiting to be seized. As the night wore on, he knew he couldn't let this chance slip away. He had come too far to be just a spectator. This was the moment to make bold choices, to step outside of his comfort zone and embrace the possibilities that lay ahead.

With newfound determination, Elliot decided to approach one of the entrances. He had to know what was happening behind those doors, even if it meant facing the uncertainty of rejection. This was his chance to seize the moment, to push his boundaries, and to start carving out his place in the world of music. As he walked toward the entrance, his heart pounding with anticipation, he couldn't help but wonder if tonight would be the turning point in his journey.

Chapter 3: Breaking the Ice

As the clock inched closer to midnight, the energy at the party shifted subtly. The initial excitement and chatter began to blend with a sense of anticipation. Elliot found himself standing at the edge of a group, half-listening to conversations while trying to maintain an air of nonchalance. The luxurious surroundings had started to feel more familiar, yet he still sensed an underlying tension among the crowd, a whisper of something greater waiting just beyond the surface.

It was during this moment of observation that a lively young woman approached him, her smile bright and infectious. "You look a bit lost," she remarked playfully, her eyes sparkling with mischief. Elliot chuckled, grateful for the distraction from his spiraling thoughts. "Just taking it all in," he replied, gesturing to the swarming masses of high-profile guests. "It's my first big event."

"Ah, a newcomer! Well, welcome to the madness." She introduced herself as Lila, a vibrant indie artist who had just landed a major collaboration. Her energy was contagious, and Elliot felt a flicker of hope ignite as they began to chat. Lila was passionate about her music and the industry, and she seemed genuinely interested in hearing his aspirations. They exchanged stories, and Elliot felt himself relax as he shared his journey as a producer.

As they talked, Lila leaned in closer, her voice dropping to a conspiratorial whisper. "You know, they say the real party starts after midnight," she said, her expression turning serious. "Only the elite few get to experience it. It's where all the real connections are made." Elliot's curiosity piqued, he leaned closer, eager for more details.

"Is that right?" he asked, his heart racing at the prospect of being part of something so exclusive. "What goes on there?"

Lila's smile widened as if she were sharing a tantalizing secret. "It's more like a gathering of the chosen ones," she explained. "The big names, the influential producers, and artists who have the power to make or break careers. If you're lucky enough to get an invite, you'll witness the magic happen."

Elliot's mind raced. This was what he had been dreaming of, an opportunity to mingle with the very people who could elevate his career to new heights. "How do I get in?" he asked, unable to hide the eagerness in his voice.

She shrugged playfully, her eyes dancing with amusement. "That's the catch. You need to know someone inside. But don't worry; I can introduce you to a few people who might have connections."

His excitement intensified. Lila's confidence made him believe that maybe he could crack into that exclusive world after all. "What's it like in there?" he probed, eager to learn more about the elusive "real party."

She hesitated for a moment, her expression thoughtful. "It's not just about the music; it's about power plays, ambition, and sometimes, a bit of chaos. You have to navigate carefully—make the right impressions, but also be prepared to hold your own. There's a lot at stake, and not everyone is friendly."

FREAK PARTY 17

Her words sent a chill down his spine, but he couldn't help but feel invigorated. This was exactly the challenge he craved, the chance to prove himself among giants.

As midnight approached, Elliot felt the pulse of the party shift once more, the air thick with excitement and possibility. He and Lila continued to chat, each word drawing him closer to the heart of the action. He could already envision himself breaking into that elite circle, rubbing shoulders with the industry's best, and finally stepping into the limelight he had worked so hard to reach.

Elliot's resolve solidified; he wouldn't just stand on the sidelines anymore. With Lila's help, he would take his first steps into the world of "the real party." The thought electrified him, fueling his ambition to break the ice and forge connections that could change everything. All he needed was one chance to show what he could bring to the table—and he was determined to seize it.

As the clock struck midnight, a ripple of excitement surged through the party, and Elliot felt the atmosphere shift yet again. The music pulsed with renewed vigor, and laughter erupted from clusters of guests who seemed to be reveling in a private joke. Just as he was beginning to feel the thrill of the night, Lila leaned in close, her voice barely above the beat.

"Let's check out that VIP room over there," she said, nodding toward a lavishly adorned door partially obscured by a curtain of shimmering beads. The door was flanked by two security guards, their expressions serious as they scanned the crowd. "I hear it's where the real action is."

AIDEN RIVERS

Elliot's heart raced at the thought. This was the opportunity he had been waiting for, yet a twinge of apprehension twisted in his gut. There was something intimidating about the exclusivity of that room—the air of mystery, the guarded nature of the guests who would be allowed inside. He hesitated, a mixture of excitement and trepidation coursing through him. What awaited him behind that door? Was it simply an elite gathering of like-minded creatives, or something more insidious?

Lila, sensing his hesitation, placed a reassuring hand on his arm. "Come on, you're not going to let a little intimidation stop you, are you?" Her smile was encouraging, but he could see a glimmer of ambition in her eyes, as if she were measuring him against her own standards. "This is the chance to meet people who can change your life. You'll regret it if you don't go in."

He took a deep breath, the sweet scent of expensive cologne and champagne swirling around him, mingling with the fragrance of the lavish floral arrangements. Elliot knew he had to push through the fear. This was a test, a rite of passage into a world he had longed to enter. If he wanted to make a name for himself, he needed to take risks—however uncomfortable they might be.

"Okay, let's do it," he said, forcing a smile and trying to shake off the nervous tension. Together, they approached the door, and as they neared, Elliot's heartbeat quickened. The bouncer, a muscular man with a no-nonsense expression, scrutinized them both. Lila flashed him a winning smile, her confidence infectious. "We're here to see the show," she declared, and Elliot nodded in agreement, trying to look as composed as possible.

FREAK PARTY

After a moment that felt like an eternity, the bouncer stepped aside, granting them access. The moment they crossed the threshold, Elliot was enveloped by a different atmosphere—more intimate, more charged with unspoken promises. The room was dimly lit, adorned with plush couches and ambient lighting that cast soft shadows across the faces of its occupants.

Inside, he spotted familiar faces—producers, artists, and celebrities, all engaged in hushed conversations that seemed to crackle with energy. A small bar was set up in one corner, and a DJ spun tracks that pulsed through the air, mixing perfectly with the sound of laughter and the clinking of glasses.

Elliot felt an immediate wave of self-doubt wash over him. Would he fit in here? Did he belong in this world of glamour and influence? As he scanned the room, he could see the easy rapport others had with one another, exchanging ideas and laughter as if they were old friends. He clutched the edge of his drink, feeling the cool glass grounding him amidst the whirlwind of emotions.

Lila, however, seemed at ease, navigating the crowd with a grace that both impressed and intimidated him. She introduced him to a few people, and Elliot made small talk, but he felt like an outsider peering into a world that was still just out of reach. Each interaction was laced with an underlying pressure to impress, to showcase his potential while simultaneously trying to blend into the fabric of this elite gathering.

His thoughts drifted back to the whispers of "the real party." What did that entail? Was this just a prelude to something more? As he stood there, a mixture of excitement and uncertainty coursing through him, he realized that he was at a crossroads.

He could either embrace the challenge or retreat to the safety of his previous existence. The decision weighed heavily on his shoulders.

In that moment, Elliot felt the urge to break the ice—to step fully into this world. He caught Lila's eye, and her encouraging nod ignited a flicker of determination within him. He would seize this moment, for better or worse, and see where it led. The night was just beginning, and he was ready to dive deeper into the thrill of possibility that lay ahead.

As Elliot stepped into the VIP room, he felt a jolt of electricity course through him, heightening his senses and awakening a thrill he hadn't anticipated. The ambiance shifted dramatically from the lively atmosphere of the main party. Here, the air was thick with an intoxicating blend of excitement and secrecy, an unspoken code that whispered of indulgence and excess. Dimmed lights danced across the room, casting long shadows that mingled with laughter and murmured conversations, making everything feel more intimate, more intense.

Elliot's gaze darted around, taking in the lavish decor—a plush carpet beneath his feet, walls adorned with abstract art that seemed to pulse with life, and plush couches that invited deep conversations. In one corner, a small group of guests leaned in close, their voices low and conspiratorial, while another group was engaged in a game that involved laughter, daring challenges, and playful shoves. The faint aroma of expensive cigars mixed with the sweetness of top-shelf liquor, a scent that was both inviting and daunting.

FREAK PARTY

He felt like he had stepped into a world that flirted with the edges of decadence—a world where rules bent and blurred under the warm glow of soft lighting. This wasn't just a gathering; it was a celebration of indulgence, a sanctuary for the bold and the brazen. As he moved further into the room, he could feel the energy pulsing around him, a magnetic pull that both exhilarated and intimidated him.

Elliot's heart raced as he spotted a couple engaged in flirtatious banter, their laughter ringing out like music. They were unabashedly close, their chemistry crackling like electricity in the air. It was a raw and unabashed display of attraction that left him slightly breathless. He marveled at their confidence, wondering if he could ever reach that level of ease in such a charged environment. Would he be able to flirt without reservation, or would he remain a hesitant observer, lingering on the sidelines?

A voice cut through his thoughts, and he turned to see a woman with striking features and an inviting smile approach him. She exuded a magnetic aura, confidence radiating from her like warmth from a flame. "Hey there, newcomer," she said, her voice smooth like silk. "What do you think of our little sanctuary?"

"Sanctuary?" he echoed, trying to match her casual demeanor, but his voice came out slightly shaky. "More like a hidden temple of indulgence."

She laughed, a sound that was rich and infectious, drawing him in. "Exactly! This is where the magic happens, away from the prying eyes of the world. You can let go of your inhibitions here. We're all friends in this room."

Elliot felt an instant connection, a spark that made his skin tingle with the thrill of possibility. They chatted, and she introduced herself as Mia, a producer known for her work in the industry. The more they talked, the more he felt a weight lift off his shoulders. Mia had an effortless charm that made him forget the pressure of making a good impression. She shared stories of her experiences, the wild moments that defined her rise in the music scene, and Elliot found himself hanging on her every word, utterly captivated.

Yet, even as the conversation flowed, he couldn't shake the feeling that something more lurked beneath the surface. He observed other guests slipping in and out of private corners, laughter mingling with hushed whispers, as if they were all part of an unspoken agreement to explore the boundaries of their desires. Elliot felt the weight of curiosity pressing on him—what were they talking about? What secrets lay behind those closed doors?

As he shared laughter with Mia, he caught glimpses of those exclusive interactions and realized he was at a crossroads. Did he want to step further into this tantalizing world? The idea thrilled him, but it also filled him with apprehension. This was a different realm, one that danced on the edges of morality and desire. He wanted to immerse himself in it, but he also felt the cautionary voice in his head reminding him to tread carefully.

Mia leaned in closer, her voice dropping to a conspiratorial whisper. "You're going to love it here, trust me. Just remember, it's all about letting go and embracing the moment. You never know what might happen."

FREAK PARTY   23

Elliot felt the pull of that moment, the seductive allure of the unknown. As he glanced around the room, he knew he was standing on the precipice of a thrilling adventure—a world where the rules of his past no longer applied. Would he dive headfirst into the depths of this elite society, or would he hold back, forever wondering what lay beyond the door? The choice loomed large, and he could feel the weight of possibility hanging in the air, daring him to break free.

Chapter 4: Seduced by Exclusivity

Elliot stood in the corner of the VIP room, watching the vibrant interplay of personalities around him. The air crackled with laughter and flirtation, a dizzying mix of confidence and allure that pulled him deeper into the scene. Despite his initial discomfort, he found himself drawn into the pulsating heart of the gathering, enchanted by the exclusive world unfolding before him. The sensation was intoxicating—a cocktail of admiration, longing, and a hint of envy for those who moved effortlessly through the crowd.

As the evening progressed, he noticed the way people gravitated toward him, their eyes sparkling with interest. Perhaps it was the newness he represented—a fresh face in a world of familiarity—or maybe it was the aura of ambition that seemed to radiate from him. Whatever it was, it flattered him, filling him with a warmth that contrasted sharply with his earlier reservations. Suddenly, he was not just a bystander; he was a participant in something bigger, something electric.

Mia returned to his side, a glass of champagne in hand. "You're fitting in nicely," she said, her tone playful yet sincere. "I told you this place was about connection. You've got something about you that draws people in."

Elliot felt heat rise to his cheeks. "Really? I didn't think anyone noticed me," he replied, a hint of disbelief lacing his words.

She laughed, her eyes sparkling with mischief. "Oh, they notice. You have that look—the look of someone who's about to break into the scene and make waves. People want to know your story. You have to lean into it."

Her words settled into him, filling him with a newfound confidence. He was part of this world, even if he had only just arrived. He scanned the room, taking in the myriad faces, some familiar and some not, all bathed in the warm glow of luxury. He felt as though he were standing at the edge of a new chapter in his life, one that could redefine everything he had ever known about the music industry and his place within it.

As if summoned by his thoughts, a couple approached, their eyes locked onto him with a mixture of curiosity and intrigue. The woman, tall and impeccably dressed in a sleek black dress, smiled warmly. "Elliot, right? I've heard about you. I'm Veronica, and this is Derek. We'd love to hear more about what you're working on."

Elliot's heart raced. He had expected small talk at best, yet here were two industry insiders seeking him out. "Oh, um, thank you!" he stammered, trying to project an air of cool composure. "I'm currently working on some new tracks—hoping to make a name for myself."

"Let's grab a seat," Derek suggested, gesturing to a nearby plush couch. "We can chat more comfortably. I'd love to hear about your vision."

As they settled in, Elliot felt the weight of their attention. He shared snippets of his aspirations, his passion evident in every word. They leaned in, encouraging him with nods and smiles that urged him to delve deeper. The thrill of being sought after, of

FREAK PARTY 27

being part of an elite conversation, swept over him, making him forget the nagging sense of discomfort that had accompanied him earlier.

In this enclave of influence and artistry, he felt powerful. This wasn't just about networking; it was about being seen, being valued. The validation sparked something deep within him, igniting a fire of ambition he hadn't realized was so dormant. The more he spoke, the more he could sense their genuine interest, their desire to connect with his ideas.

As the conversation flowed, he couldn't help but glance around the room, absorbing the grandeur of it all. The laughter felt louder, the music seemed to pulse in rhythm with his heartbeat, and the atmosphere buzzed with potential. He could taste the exclusivity, the promise of something exhilarating just beneath the surface. This was the world he had dreamed of, a world where boundaries faded, and ambition soared.

Yet, as the excitement enveloped him, he couldn't shake the sensation that there was more to this elite gathering than met the eye. There were layers beneath the polished conversations and the sparkling laughter—layers that hinted at indulgences and secrets he had yet to uncover. But in that moment, amidst the laughter and allure, Elliot found himself leaning into the moment, ready to embrace whatever came next.

As Elliot immersed himself in the electric atmosphere of the VIP room, he felt an undeniable shift in how others perceived him. The influential figures surrounding him radiated an aura of importance and power, and somehow, in this swirling sea of elite personalities, he found himself being accepted, welcomed into a circle he had only dreamed of entering.

Veronica and Derek had introduced him to a few key players in the industry. One such figure was Alexei Moreau, a renowned music producer whose very name evoked whispers of success. Tall and impeccably dressed, Alexei had an air of authority that drew people in. His reputation for spotting talent was legendary, and as he extended his hand to Elliot, the younger man felt the weight of that moment settle heavily on his shoulders.

"Elliot, is it? I've heard interesting things about your work," Alexei said, his voice smooth like the finest silk. "I'd love to hear more about what you're creating."

Elliot felt a surge of adrenaline at the invitation. "Thank you! I'm working on a few tracks that blend different genres. I want to push boundaries, bring something fresh to the table," he replied, his voice steady despite the flutter in his chest. The moment felt surreal; here he was, discussing his dreams with a man whose accolades adorned the walls of every major record label.

As the conversation flowed, Elliot shared snippets of his latest project, each word drawing Alexei's gaze closer. He explained his vision for a collaboration that fused electronic beats with classic instrumentation, aiming to create a sound that resonated deeply with listeners. With every nod and intrigued expression from Alexei, Elliot's confidence soared. He could see the wheels turning in the producer's mind, perhaps even imagining how Elliot's ambition might fit into the larger narrative of the music industry.

"Sounds promising," Alexei remarked, leaning in slightly, his interest piqued. "It's refreshing to meet someone with such passion. We need more of that in this industry." Elliot's heart raced at the validation. He was not just another aspiring producer; in this moment, he was someone worth listening to.

FREAK PARTY 29

Soon after, another prominent figure approached—Isabella Chen, a fiercely independent artist known for her bold sound and unapologetic lyrics. Isabella was a force to be reckoned with, her presence commanding attention. She was both intimidating and captivating, a woman who had carved out her niche in an industry that often stifled originality.

"Elliot, right?" she said, her voice cutting through the chatter like a blade. "I've heard your name tossed around a bit. What's your angle?"

Surprised but excited, Elliot replied, "I'm trying to create music that speaks to real experiences, something that resonates on a deeper level. I believe we can push the envelope."

Isabella raised an eyebrow, impressed. "That's what we need more of—realness. Let's see where your ideas can take you," she said, a hint of a challenge in her tone. The thrill of her approval sent shivers down his spine. Being noticed by such a renowned artist felt like validation, as if he were being invited into a secret club where only the most innovative and daring members resided.

As the night unfolded, Elliot found himself mingling with others who shared similar sentiments, each interaction reinforcing his burgeoning sense of self-worth. Conversations flowed like the champagne that filled their glasses, each moment punctuated with laughter and camaraderie. He felt buoyed by the knowledge that these established figures were not just hearing him; they were engaging with his ideas, considering him an equal, if only for this fleeting night.

However, beneath the glimmering surface, Elliot couldn't shake the feeling that something more was at play. The exclusivity of the event, the weight of the connections he was forming—it all felt layered, as if there were unspoken rules he hadn't yet grasped. The laughter echoed in his ears, and he wondered how far he could go in this world that had so quickly wrapped around him.

Yet, the seduction of the moment was intoxicating. He basked in the glow of attention, relishing the feeling of being seen and acknowledged by those he had long admired. In this place, he was no longer just a young music producer from a small town; he was a potential player in the grand game of the music industry, and he was determined to seize every opportunity that lay before him.

As he navigated through the crowd, a sense of belonging began to bloom within him. Each smile, each compliment, and every nod of approval felt like a step further into a world that was beginning to feel like home. The evening was still young, and Elliot couldn't help but wonder what other revelations awaited him in the depths of this exclusive gathering.

As the night deepened, Elliot found himself increasingly ensconced in the swirling conversations that flowed like the champagne circulating through the room. The air was thick with an intoxicating blend of ambition, laughter, and a palpable undercurrent of intrigue that pulled him in. He listened intently, occasionally contributing to discussions that spanned everything from the latest music trends to whispered anecdotes about the industry's elite. But beneath the surface of pleasantries, he sensed something deeper—an unspoken understanding among the guests, a silent code that hinted at the darker side of this glamorous world.

FREAK PARTY 31

It began with a casual remark from Isabella, her laughter ringing out as she recounted a wild night at a previous afterparty. "You never really know what you're getting into, do you? The real fun happens when the lights go down," she said, her tone conspiratorial. The group erupted in laughter, but Elliot noticed a flicker of something else in their eyes—an acknowledgment of secrets that lay beyond the glittering façade. He could feel the weight of their words hanging in the air, a thread pulling him closer to an undisclosed narrative.

Elliot tried to maintain his composure, wanting to join in on the excitement, yet a knot formed in his stomach. What was the "real fun" they were alluding to? He hesitated to probe further, caught between the thrill of acceptance and the instinctual wariness of what might be revealed. He had come here to forge connections, to network and position himself in the industry, not to uncover hidden truths that could threaten the allure of the evening. The last thing he wanted was to appear naive or overly inquisitive.

However, curiosity gnawed at him. He watched as other guests exchanged knowing glances, their smiles tinged with mischief. A few whispered together, their voices barely above a murmur, as if speaking in a language that only they understood. The laughter turned conspiratorial, and the atmosphere shifted slightly, as if the room itself had been sealed off from the outside world. He noticed the way they moved, subtly guided by an unseen hand, shifting toward the edges of the room where the more secluded seating was located.

As he turned back to his conversation with Alexei, he felt the producer's gaze drift toward the corner of the room, where shadows danced, hinting at deeper mysteries. "Elliot, you're going to want to keep your ear to the ground. In this industry, the lines between what's acceptable and what's not can blur rather quickly," Alexei advised, his voice low, yet firm. Elliot felt a chill run down his spine at the implications behind those words.

"Are you suggesting there's more to this party than meets the eye?" Elliot ventured, trying to sound casual.

"Let's just say there are certain circles that don't take kindly to outsiders. But if you play your cards right, you might just find yourself on the inside," Alexei replied, his smirk both enticing and cryptic. The double entendre hung heavy in the air, and Elliot's pulse quickened as he considered the possibilities. He knew he had a choice to make—embrace the thrill of the unknown or tread carefully along the fringes.

Around them, conversations grew bolder, laced with flirtation and intrigue. A group gathered nearby, laughter bubbling over as one guest shared a story that culminated in a wink and an implication of secret indulgences only whispered among the elite. The laughter that followed held an edge, as if they were reveling in a shared understanding that excluded anyone not "in the know." Elliot felt a twinge of discomfort as he observed their interactions, the intimacy forged in shared secrets.

He glanced toward the closed doors lining the back of the room, guarded by watchful security personnel, and a thrill of fear mingled with excitement raced through him. What lay beyond those doors? Was this where the real festivities began, where boundaries faded and the elite indulged in their darker desires? Elliot had always been a curious soul, but at this moment, the weight of the unknown pressed down upon him.

FREAK PARTY

Still, he hesitated. The prospect of crossing that threshold held both promise and peril. Was he ready to dive into this world where the lines of morality were obscured by the glamour that surrounded him? Part of him was captivated by the idea of being part of something so exclusive, while another part whispered caution.

In that tension, Elliot found himself at a crossroads, teetering between the allure of acceptance and the instinct to protect himself from the potential fallout. He was still the aspiring producer, yearning for success, but he could feel the tantalizing seduction of the night tugging at him, urging him to step deeper into the shadows where the true essence of this world lay hidden.

Chapter 5: The Rumours

Elliot stood near the bar, his half-empty glass of champagne shimmering under the dim lights, reflecting the vibrant energy of the party around him. He had spent the last hour mingling and attempting to navigate the complex social landscape, but now he found himself more intrigued than ever by the whispered conversations echoing through the opulent space. The air was thick with the promise of secrets, and Elliot felt like an outsider peering into a world that was just out of reach.

As he leaned in to listen more closely, he overheard two guests, a striking woman in a shimmering silver gown and a tall man in a tailored suit, engaged in a hushed conversation. Their voices were low, but the tone was laced with excitement, punctuated by glances around the room as if they were ensuring no one else could hear.

"Did you hear about last week's afterparty?" the woman asked, her eyes sparkling with mischief. "They say it got wild—people getting into things that are usually kept behind closed doors."

Elliot's heart raced at the mention of "afterparty." It was clear that this gathering was not merely a collection of industry professionals celebrating their successes. There were layers to this world, shadows lurking just beneath the surface, and he wanted to know more.

"What did they do this time?" the man replied, leaning in closer, his expression eager.

She smirked, a knowing smile that hinted at knowledge only shared among the most privileged. "You know how it goes. A little bit of everything—excess, indulgence, and some rather... risqué activities. The kind of stuff that would make a headline if it ever got out."

Elliot felt a thrill at the thought. This was the realm he had dreamed of—the world where art and ambition collided with a hint of danger. He couldn't help but feel a pull towards this darker side of the industry. Yet, he also felt a wave of apprehension. Was he prepared to step into such a world? What kind of price did one pay for acceptance among this elite group?

The woman continued, her voice a mix of conspiratorial excitement and caution. "They have their insiders—people who know how to keep their mouths shut. But there are always rumours, and you know how quickly those can spread."

Rumours. The word echoed in Elliot's mind. It was both enticing and daunting. He had heard whispers about the industry's darker corners, but hearing it in this context made it feel more real, more immediate. He glanced around the room, taking in the faces of those who were mingling, laughing, and enjoying the high life. He felt a desire to be part of their world, but the stories he had heard also filled him with uncertainty.

"Honestly, I don't think I could handle it," the man said, shaking his head, but there was a flicker of intrigue in his eyes. "What if someone snaps a photo? You'd be finished."

FREAK PARTY 37

The woman laughed lightly, tossing her hair over her shoulder. "Oh, darling, it's all about knowing who to trust. There are plenty of cameras here tonight, but those who truly belong have ways of navigating around them."

Elliot's thoughts raced. He felt the weight of their words pressing upon him. He had come here seeking connections and potential opportunities, but the idea of being drawn into a world where discretion was paramount made his pulse quicken. He was no stranger to the concept of exclusivity, but this was something entirely different.

Just then, the conversation shifted as the pair turned their attention to a group of high-profile guests entering the room. The sight sent a ripple of excitement through the crowd, and Elliot couldn't help but feel a sense of urgency building within him. He had to find a way to break through the superficial layers of this party and learn more about the hidden dynamics that seemed to govern the interactions around him.

He took a deep breath, his gaze sweeping the room. If he wanted to be a part of this world, he would need to immerse himself fully in it. This was a test, a chance to step beyond the façade and understand the intricate web of relationships that could make or break his career. Would he have the courage to pursue the whispers of rumors and navigate the complexities of this elite circle? The night was still young, and he felt a fire igniting within him, driving him forward into the heart of the mystery that lay before him.

Elliot felt an urgency coursing through him, propelling him to seek answers to the mysteries whispered among the partygoers. He spotted Jenna, a friendly acquaintance he had met earlier in the evening while admiring a stunning piece of art that adorned the venue's wall. She had been animated and welcoming, her laughter infectious as she shared anecdotes about her own experiences in the industry. Now, she seemed like the perfect person to help him unravel the threads of gossip that had piqued his curiosity.

He made his way through the crowd, the muffled sounds of laughter and clinking glasses creating an intoxicating symphony that heightened his senses. The atmosphere felt charged, and the air was thick with secrets. Elliot found Jenna leaning against the bar, a vibrant cocktail in hand, her expression glowing under the soft lighting. She caught his eye and smiled warmly, inviting him into her orbit.

"Hey, Jenna!" he said, forcing a casual tone as he approached her. "Can I steal you for a second?"

"Of course! What's up?" she replied, her eyes sparkling with interest.

Elliot hesitated for a moment, trying to frame his question without sounding too desperate or naive. "I overheard some people talking about the afterparty and some of the, uh, activities that go on. I'm curious if you could tell me more about it."

The moment the words left his lips, he saw a flicker of surprise cross her face, quickly replaced by a veil of guardedness. "Oh, you know how it is," she said, shrugging lightly as if brushing off his inquiry. "People like to embellish stories. It's all part of the game."

He could sense her evasiveness and pressed on. "But you're in the industry. I thought you might have some insight. Is it really as wild as they say?"

FREAK PARTY 39

Jenna took a sip of her drink, her gaze drifting away for a moment as she considered her response. "Listen, Elliot, the parties can get a bit crazy, but it's not like what you might be imagining. Most of it is just... networking. Everyone's trying to make connections and find their way up the ladder."

"Networking?" he repeated, feeling the tension in his chest tighten. "Is that what they call it?"

Her eyes darted around the room, checking for eavesdroppers. "You know, people talk. But not everyone is in it for the same reasons. Some are just here to enjoy themselves, while others are looking to take advantage of the situation. It's a mixed bag."

Elliot leaned closer, intrigued yet wary. "What about those rumours? The secretive stuff?" He could feel his heart racing, the thrill of the chase urging him to dig deeper. "Surely you've heard something."

"Honestly, it's best not to get involved in those kinds of conversations," she replied, her tone now a mixture of caution and concern. "Trust me, you don't want to find yourself caught up in something that could backfire. The industry can be brutal, and people have long memories."

Elliot felt a pang of disappointment. He had hoped Jenna would offer him the inside scoop, a glimpse into the tantalizing world that lay just beyond his reach. Instead, he was left with more questions and a lingering feeling of unease. He sensed that there was a delicate balance at play, one that he was not yet equipped to navigate.

"Right," he said, forcing a smile. "I guess it's all part of the allure, huh?"

"Exactly," she said, her demeanor brightening slightly. "It's exciting to be here, but just remember to keep your wits about you. Some doors are better left unopened."

Elliot nodded, feeling a mix of frustration and fascination. He wasn't ready to let go of the intrigue that surrounded him. He wanted to push past the superficial layers of the party and discover what lay beneath the surface. There had to be more to it than mere networking and polite conversation.

As Jenna turned to greet someone else, Elliot stepped back, trying to process what he had learned. He could sense the pulse of the party around him, a dynamic blend of ambition and ambition masked by laughter and glitz. He knew he had to find a way to understand the unspoken rules of this elite world, to learn how to walk the fine line between ambition and naivety.

He glanced around, spotting the same two guests from earlier, still deep in conversation. There was something magnetic about their exchange, a hidden knowledge that beckoned to him. Taking a deep breath, he decided he would not let this opportunity slip away. He would find another way to break through the facade and learn the secrets that thrummed beneath the surface of the evening's festivities. After all, the night was still young, and he was determined to unearth the truths that danced just beyond his grasp.

The buzz of excitement thrummed in the air, yet it was laced with an undertone of secrecy that Elliot couldn't shake. As he wandered deeper into the party, he felt like an outsider peering into a world brimming with hidden dangers and clandestine activities. The whispers he had overheard were like shadows lurking just out of sight, and a growing curiosity compelled him to investigate further.

FREAK PARTY 41

Elliot made his way through the crowd, keenly aware of the faces around him. He noted the way conversations abruptly hushed when newcomers approached, and how laughter faded to murmurs that seemed to pulse with the rhythm of the party. His heart raced with anticipation and trepidation. He needed to find out more about the secretive allure of "the real party" that others had hinted at but never fully revealed.

Feeling emboldened, he decided to break away from the throngs of people sipping champagne and exchanging pleasantries. He navigated his way toward a dimly lit corridor at the far end of the venue, where the atmosphere shifted from exuberance to something more charged, almost electric. The flickering lights and muffled music behind closed doors drew him in, creating a magnetic pull he couldn't resist.

As he approached one of the doors, he paused, unsure of what he might find inside. Voices floated out, animated and tinged with excitement, but the conversations were too muffled to decipher. He could sense the weight of anticipation in the air, thick and heady like the scent of expensive cologne and perfume that lingered in the corridor. Elliot's instincts urged him to step closer, to lean in and eavesdrop on the secrets that lay just beyond his reach.

With a deep breath, he edged nearer, his heart pounding as he strained to hear. The laughter within sounded unrestrained, punctuated by what he thought might be the clink of glasses or even something more illicit. It was a different world beyond this threshold, one that beckoned him with promises of excitement and adventure.

Before he could second-guess himself, Elliot pushed the door open just a crack, allowing himself a glimpse into the room. The sight that met his eyes sent a thrill racing through him. The space was illuminated by soft, ambient lights that cast alluring shadows on the walls, revealing a luxurious lounge filled with plush furniture. People lounged on velvet sofas, their body language intimate and inviting, yet the tension in the air was palpable.

Elliot could see a group of guests huddled closely, exchanging conspiratorial glances and hushed laughter, their demeanor strikingly different from the casual elegance of the main party. It was as if he had stumbled upon a hidden enclave, where rules were forgotten and the thrill of the forbidden danced like smoke in the air.

Sensing an urgency, he pushed the door open wider, revealing a scene that was both intoxicating and intimidating. The guests inside looked up, their eyes narrowing as they registered his presence. Elliot's heart raced, a mixture of excitement and anxiety flooding his senses. He was an outsider, a newcomer encroaching on sacred territory.

"Who are you?" one of the guests asked, their tone a mix of curiosity and suspicion. The question hung in the air like a challenge, igniting a spark of defiance within Elliot. He had come too far to retreat now.

"Just someone looking to learn more about the party," he replied, trying to sound casual despite the rapid beat of his heart. "I heard whispers about something more... exclusive happening here."

FREAK PARTY 43

The room fell silent, tension hanging thick in the air. Elliot's pulse quickened as the group exchanged glances, their expressions unreadable. It was clear they were weighing his presence, assessing whether to embrace him or push him back into the shadows from which he'd emerged.

Finally, a woman with striking features and an air of confidence stepped forward, a smirk playing on her lips. "You want to know what's really going on here?" she asked, her voice dripping with intrigue. "Then you'd better be ready for what lies ahead. Not everyone who enters this world comes out unscathed."

Elliot swallowed hard, his resolve hardening. He was in too deep to turn back now. "I'm ready," he declared, determination igniting within him. The allure of the hidden party promised something exhilarating, and he was willing to risk it all to uncover the truth. The night was far from over, and he was about to embark on a journey that would lead him into the heart of secrets he had only dared to imagine.

With a nod from the woman, he stepped fully into the room, ready to embrace the darkness that lay ahead. The door closed behind him, sealing his fate as he crossed the threshold into a world that would test his limits and redefine everything he thought he knew about ambition, desire, and the cost of exclusivity.

Chapter 6: The Revelation

The energy in the VIP room crackled around Elliot, each whisper and glance charged with unspoken secrets. As the conversations around him escalated, he could feel the weight of their indulgence pressing in on him. He was both exhilarated and terrified, caught between the allure of what he was witnessing and the stark reality of what it meant. He needed answers.

Finding his friend from earlier, a woman named Jade who had been warm and welcoming, he pulled her aside, desperate for clarity amidst the chaos. Her sharp eyes flickered with amusement and concern as he leaned in closer, determined to uncover the truth.

"Jade, can you tell me what's really going on here? I keep hearing things—rumors about these parties being different than what they seem." His voice was steady, but he felt a tremor of apprehension beneath the surface.

She laughed softly, a sound that danced in the air between them. "Different? That's one way to put it. But you have to understand, Elliot, these parties are not just about music and connections. They're... notorious."

"Notorious?" he echoed, confusion and curiosity mixing in his chest. "What do you mean?"

Jade glanced around, ensuring they were not overheard before leaning in closer, her expression serious. "The mogul's parties are famous for their hedonistic indulgence. It's not just a gathering of artists and industry giants; it's a playground for the elite. There's a lot of... excess involved."

Elliot felt a chill run down his spine as her words sank in. The extravagant displays of wealth, the decadent atmosphere—it was all starting to make a disturbing kind of sense. "Excess?" he repeated, his heart racing. "Like what?"

Jade hesitated, her gaze flickering with hesitation before she pressed on. "People come here to escape, to explore their desires without judgment. You'll see things you might not be prepared for. Drugs, illicit affairs... It's all part of the allure. The mogul caters to the whims of his guests, providing an experience that's impossible to find elsewhere."

Elliot's mind spun at the implications of her revelation. He had come seeking opportunities, hoping to forge connections that would propel his career forward, but now he was faced with a world that could easily consume him. "And you're okay with this?" he asked, bewildered by the casual way she spoke about such dangerous behavior.

She shrugged, a flicker of defiance in her eyes. "I'm not here to judge. Everyone makes their own choices, right? You can choose to partake or just enjoy the spectacle. It's your decision. But know that once you step into this world, there's no going back."

He stared at her, absorbing the weight of her words. The realization of the stakes involved began to settle in, yet he couldn't shake the feeling of exhilaration that pulsed beneath

FREAK PARTY

his apprehension. This was a rare opportunity, one that could catapult him into the stratosphere of the industry, yet it also threatened to drown him in chaos.

"What about you?" he pressed, genuinely curious about her perspective. "How do you navigate it all? Don't you ever feel like you're losing control?"

Jade smiled, but it was tinged with something darker. "Control is an illusion, Elliot. This place teaches you that quickly. You either embrace the chaos or let it overwhelm you. I've chosen to ride the wave, to see where it takes me. But remember, not everyone is cut out for this life."

Her words hung heavily in the air as Elliot processed them. The hedonistic lifestyle sounded intoxicating and dangerous, a sharp contrast to the polished façade he had admired upon arrival. Yet, he felt an undeniable draw toward it, a magnetic pull that whispered of indulgence and liberation.

As the music thumped around them, drawing in waves of laughter and energy, Elliot felt a pulse in his veins that matched the rhythm. The revelation had shattered the illusion of glamor he had held onto, but it also ignited a fire within him. He was on the precipice of something monumental, and he had to decide whether to leap into the unknown or retreat to the safety of his former life.

His thoughts raced as he glanced back at the crowd, the laughter and chaos beckoning him. This was his moment, a chance to dive deeper into a world that promised both peril and possibility. The night was far from over, and he could either walk away or plunge headfirst into the abyss.

AIDEN RIVERS

Elliot stepped away from Jade, his mind a whirlwind of conflicting emotions. The revelations about the mogul's parties spun in his head like a frenetic dance, leaving him both excited and anxious. He glanced around the VIP room, taking in the revelers who laughed and toasted with abandon, seemingly unaware of the shadows lurking just beyond their bright lights.

Rationality kicked in as he leaned against the plush wall, trying to brush off the rumors that had seeped into his consciousness. Maybe Jade was exaggerating; after all, she thrived in this world of opulence. Surely, the whispers of hedonism and excess were just part of the scene, embellished tales meant to add allure to an already extravagant affair.

He took a deep breath, willing himself to relax. *Focus on the music, the people. This is your chance.* He closed his eyes for a moment, the pulsing beats reverberating through his chest, coaxing him back into the thrill of the night. He had worked too hard to get here, to turn his back now over a few ominous whispers.

But as he opened his eyes and surveyed the room, he could still feel the unease lingering in his gut. His mind flickered back to Jade's words, the way she had spoken about indulgence and the darker side of this elite circle. It wasn't just the drugs or the flings that unsettled him; it was the notion that there were boundaries being pushed—moral lines that, once crossed, could lead to places he might not want to go.

He found himself drifting toward a group of partygoers gathered around a small table laden with an assortment of drinks and a few unfamiliar substances that glimmered under the dim lights. Their laughter rang out, carefree and loud, contrasting

FREAK PARTY

sharply with the gnawing apprehension knotting in his stomach. Elliot's instinct urged him to join in, to blend with the revelers and forget the shadows, yet something held him back.

"What are you drinking?" a voice broke through his thoughts. A tall man with a sharp jaw and striking blue eyes approached, his smile inviting yet predatory. "You look like you could use something to take the edge off."

Elliot hesitated, glancing at the man's hand, which cradled a crystal glass filled with a vibrant liquid that caught the light in a way that made it look otherworldly. He knew he should be cautious, but the man's charisma was hard to resist. "Um, just a soda for now," Elliot replied, trying to keep his tone casual, though he could feel the tension radiating off him.

"Suit yourself. But trust me, you'll want to try something stronger if you want to enjoy the night." The man's smile widened, and Elliot felt a chill run down his spine. Was this how things worked in this world—surrendering your will to fit in?

As the man sauntered away, Elliot was left to grapple with his conflicting feelings. He glanced back at Jade, who was now engaged in animated conversation with a couple of other guests, their laughter ringing out like a siren's call. There was a part of him that craved that kind of carefree existence, one where the stakes didn't feel so high. But another part—more instinctual and protective—warned him to tread lightly.

He turned back to the crowd, trying to shake off the creeping doubt. *Just enjoy yourself,* he told himself. He had worked hard to get this far, and he wasn't about to let rumors dictate his experience. But every time he caught a glimpse of the guarded

VIP rooms, or heard a laugh that seemed tinged with something darker, his unease flared up again, reminding him that not everything was as it seemed.

Elliot wandered further into the throng, searching for a distraction, for something—anything—that could drown out the whispers of risk swirling around him. He found himself near the dance floor, where bodies moved fluidly to the music, lost in a collective rhythm. He felt the pulse of the night beneath his feet and decided to join in, letting the beat wash over him as he surrendered to the moment.

But even as he danced, a part of him remained alert, conscious of the hidden dynamics at play in the room. The rumors lingered in his mind like smoke, elusive yet ever-present, a reminder that in this world of glitz and glamour, darkness often lurked just below the surface. Would he allow himself to get lost in it, or would he fight to retain his sense of self amid the seductive chaos? The question loomed over him as the night wore on, leaving him to grapple with the choice he would soon have to make.

Elliot stood at the periphery of the dance floor, feeling the music vibrate through his body while his mind struggled to make sense of the swirling chaos around him. The vibrant lights pulsed in time with the beat, but his gaze drifted away from the carefree movements of the guests to the more subtle actions occurring just beyond the crowd.

His attention was drawn to a group gathered at the far end of the VIP area, their laughter sharp and conspiratorial. They leaned in close, their body language charged with a mix of secrecy and excitement. Elliot strained to catch snippets of their conversation, and a chill ran down his spine when he overheard

FREAK PARTY 51

phrases that echoed the rumors he had been trying to dismiss. Words like "afterparty" and "exclusive" floated through the air, punctuated by knowing glances that seemed to communicate far more than mere words.

With his heart racing, Elliot leaned in, pretending to engage with the dance crowd while secretly observing the group. One man, tall and lean with a confident posture, held a drink in one hand while the other gestured animatedly as if revealing a great secret. His words were too muffled by the music for Elliot to decipher, but the way the others leaned in closer, their expressions shifting from amusement to intrigue, left an impression of something more serious and dangerous.

He noticed another figure, a woman with striking features and a magnetic aura, subtly slipping something into her purse while exchanging a quick glance with the tall man. The action was discreet, but to Elliot, it felt like a revelation in itself. *What are they doing?* The realization that they might be engaging in something illicit sent a wave of unease washing over him. This was not just a party; it was a world where secrets were currency, and the rules felt dangerously flexible.

Feeling increasingly isolated amidst the sea of revelry, Elliot's pulse quickened as he began to question everything. He had envisioned this night as a stepping stone, a chance to network with the influential figures of the music industry, but now he found himself entangled in a web of uncertainty. What had he truly signed up for? Was he ready to dive into this underworld of privilege and pleasure, or would he emerge with his integrity intact?

As he scanned the room, Elliot spotted Jade mingling effortlessly, a cocktail in one hand and laughter spilling from her lips. She seemed unfazed by the tension that had begun to coil around him. Did she know about the darker elements lurking beneath the surface? Was she part of it? He recalled their earlier conversation, her flirtation with the idea of indulgence, and felt a pang of betrayal, wondering if he had misjudged her motives.

Suddenly, a sense of urgency surged within him. If he didn't act soon, he risked being swept into this world where boundaries blurred and shadows loomed. He had come to this party seeking opportunity, but now it felt like a gamble with his very identity at stake.

Elliot took a deep breath and stepped back from the crowd, wanting to retreat from the growing tension. He needed clarity, a moment to process what was unfolding around him. The excitement of the party had shifted into something more sinister, and he felt like a fish out of water, struggling to breathe in an environment that had suddenly turned murky.

As he stepped into a quieter corner of the room, he glanced back at the group, now engaged in hushed conversation again. Their laughter echoed with a different timbre, one that felt more exclusive, more dangerous. He could sense the invisible wall that separated him from them, a barrier built on knowledge and experience that he didn't yet possess.

The world he had stepped into was intoxicating and alluring, but beneath its glossy surface lay shadows that whispered of temptation and consequence. Elliot closed his eyes momentarily, fighting to quell the rising tide of apprehension. He had to decide whether to dive deeper or pull back, but the choice felt more daunting than ever. In this game of music, fame, and hidden desires, the stakes were rising, and he was about to discover just how perilous the path ahead could be.

Chapter 7: Behind Closed Doors

Elliot's heart raced as he clutched the slip of paper that granted him access to the afterparty area. The atmosphere buzzed with anticipation, a blend of glamour and something darker lurking just beneath the surface. As he stepped through the velvet ropes, the dim lighting enveloped him, casting shadows that danced along the walls and whispered promises of indulgence.

The room was opulent yet strangely suffocating. Plush couches and artful decorations adorned the space, creating an illusion of comfort that belied the tension in the air. Elliot's pulse quickened as he surveyed the scene, trying to shake off the unease gnawing at his insides. This was not the environment he had envisioned; the glamorous aura felt tainted, infused with a sense of recklessness he hadn't anticipated.

He moved further inside, drawn in by the alluring melodies and laughter echoing off the walls. But as he approached the heart of the afterparty, the activities on display left him feeling both fascinated and repulsed. Groups gathered in clusters, their conversations hushed yet charged with energy. As he observed more closely, Elliot's stomach dropped at the realization that the playful chatter was often accompanied by touches that blurred the line of consent, glances laden with unspoken desires, and gestures that hinted at an unrestrained hedonism.

A tall figure caught his eye—a woman draped in a shimmering silver dress that clung to her curves as she laughed, her laughter tinkling like glass. She was entangled in conversation with a prominent producer, their bodies swaying dangerously close. Elliot recognized him from various industry events, a man whose name was synonymous with both brilliance and scandal. He had always respected the man's work but was now confronted with the uncomfortable knowledge of what might be hidden behind his polished persona.

The sight of the duo exchanging flirtations sent a chill through Elliot. He couldn't shake the feeling that this was a place where morals shifted, where ambition could easily slip into exploitation. The allure of success seemed to hang in the air, intoxicating those who sought it, but the cost felt heavier than he had imagined. His upbringing had instilled in him a strong set of values, and witnessing this unfolding debauchery struck a discordant note in his soul.

As he turned to leave the scene, he nearly collided with a group sharing a bottle of champagne, their laughter piercing through his thoughts. One of the women leaned into him, her breath laced with alcohol, as she playfully pushed him toward the group. "Join us! Don't be such a wallflower!" she insisted, her eyes twinkling with mischief. Elliot forced a smile, trying to shake off the tightness in his chest. *This isn't me,* he reminded himself. *I came here to make connections, not to become part of this.* Yet the pressure to conform was palpable, a weight pressing down on him as he considered the potential networking opportunities slipping away.

FREAK PARTY 57

He stepped back, seeking refuge in the periphery once more. His gaze swept across the room, landing on a corner where two men whispered closely, their demeanor tense. As they parted, Elliot caught a glimpse of a small, folded piece of paper being exchanged between them. The act seemed innocuous at first, but something in the way they looked around before passing it sent alarm bells ringing in Elliot's mind.

What had he stumbled into? This was not merely a party; it was a showcase of power, influence, and the darker facets of the industry he had long admired. The glamour he had yearned for now felt tainted by the shadows creeping in around him. He sensed that behind the façade of exclusivity lay hidden dangers that he was not prepared to face.

Taking a deep breath, Elliot reminded himself of his goals. He wanted to make a name for himself in music, not become another story whispered in the dark. Yet, the allure of the elite circle around him was undeniable, and he found himself grappling with conflicting desires—an eagerness to belong and a fierce determination to remain true to himself. As he stood at the precipice of this new world, Elliot knew that he had to tread carefully, for one misstep could lead him down a path he may never return from.

As Elliot stepped deeper into the afterparty, the ambience shifted from casual revelry to an electric tension that buzzed in the air. The elite circles that congregated here radiated an unspoken power. He moved with a cautious curiosity, feeling the weight of expectations pressing against him. Just ahead, a cluster of sharply dressed individuals held court in a secluded area, their laughter mingling with conspiratorial whispers that beckoned him closer.

He was approached by a tall man, impeccably tailored in a suit that exuded both confidence and authority. The man's presence was magnetic, and as he introduced himself as Victor, a well-known talent manager, Elliot felt an immediate pull. "I've seen you around," Victor said, his voice smooth like silk. "You've got potential. We could do great things together."

Elliot's heart raced at the prospect. This was the kind of opportunity he had long dreamed of, but as Victor leaned closer, a disquieting edge crept into the conversation. "We're not just here for the music, you know," he continued, his tone shifting to a more serious note. "In this world, it's about connections—powerful connections. The kind that can help you soar or sink you into obscurity."

Elliot's pulse quickened as Victor laid out an enticing offer: exclusive deals, introductions to high-profile clients, and a promise of stardom that seemed almost too good to be true. Yet, alongside the allure came an unsettling expectation—a silent pact that demanded loyalty and discretion. Victor leaned in, lowering his voice conspiratorially. "What happens behind closed doors stays behind closed doors. Understand?"

A wave of apprehension washed over Elliot. The words hung in the air, heavy with implications. Loyalty? Silence? The thrill of opportunity was quickly overshadowed by a sense of foreboding. What exactly was he being drawn into? He hesitated, searching for the right response, but the room pulsed with a mix of desperation and ambition, and his head swirled with the possibilities that lay before him.

As he processed Victor's proposition, the attention of the room shifted. Other guests, drawn in by the conversation, began to gather. Each face was familiar in the industry, some adorned

FREAK PARTY 59

with accolades, others tainted by rumors. Elliot felt the weight of their gazes, an invisible pressure urging him to make a choice, to align himself with this powerful faction.

Another figure, a woman with striking green eyes and an enigmatic smile, stepped forward. "You're talented, Elliot," she said, her voice sultry yet commanding. "But talent alone won't get you far here. It's about who you know and what you're willing to do." She held out her hand, revealing a card that shimmered in the low light. "If you're interested, we can help each other."

Elliot's mind raced as he glanced at the card, his heart pounding in his chest. It was an invitation to a world that was both alluring and terrifying. The thought of finally breaking into the inner circle ignited a flicker of excitement within him, but the shadows of doubt lingered. Was this the path he truly wanted to take? The idea of trading his principles for connections felt like a dangerous game.

As Victor continued to outline the benefits of joining their ranks, Elliot felt a surge of anxiety. He wanted to make a name for himself, but at what cost? He recalled his dreams of creating music that resonated with authenticity, not one tinged with the compromises he now faced. But the more Victor spoke, the more tempting the promise of success became.

"Join us, and you won't just be a name in the credits," Victor urged, his intensity palpable. "You'll be a force in this industry. Your sound, your vision—everyone will know your name."

The voices around him blurred, becoming a cacophony of ambition and desire. Elliot felt as if he were standing at a precipice, with the allure of a new world laid out before him. But the deeper he delved into this world of elite connections, the more he sensed the strings attached. Was he prepared to navigate the murky waters of fame, where loyalty and silence could be the price of entry?

As the night wore on, Elliot grappled with his decision. Each whispered promise felt like a thread binding him to this dangerous game, and he couldn't shake the feeling that stepping through this door might lead him to a place from which he could never return. With every beat of his heart, the pull of exclusivity tightened its grip, and Elliot was left wondering if he had the strength to resist the seductive call of power.

Elliot stood in the pulsating heart of the afterparty, feeling like a moth drawn to a flame, yet acutely aware of the impending burn. The glitzy allure of power and success was intoxicating, but as he listened to Victor and the others, he grappled with a rising tide of unease. It was a heady cocktail of ambition and anxiety, and each moment spent in this world made him acutely aware of the thin line he was teetering on.

The laughter around him felt hollow, echoing against the walls that seemed to close in with every passing second. He took a step back, glancing around at the guests who were absorbed in their own indulgences. Each face reflected a different story of ambition, pleasure, and, perhaps, desperation. As he observed them, he felt a pang of doubt—was he prepared to sacrifice his values to join their ranks? The siren song of success whispered sweetly, but it was laced with the bitterness of compromise.

He remembered why he had come here in the first place: the music, the artistry, the dream of creating something meaningful. But now, standing among these powerful figures, the weight of their expectations pressed heavily upon him. The thrill of potential fame was overshadowed by the reality of what he would need to do to achieve it. He could almost hear the echoes of his conscience warning him against becoming another faceless name in a sea of compromised ideals.

"Elliot, you okay?" Victor's voice broke through his reverie, laced with a hint of concern. "You seem a bit lost."

"I'm just... processing everything," Elliot replied, forcing a smile that felt like a mask over his turmoil. "It's a lot to take in."

Victor studied him for a moment, a knowing look passing over his features. "This is just the beginning, my friend. It's all about choices. You can either seize this opportunity or let it slip away." He leaned closer, his voice dropping to a conspiratorial whisper. "But know that the game requires a certain mindset. If you want to play, you've got to commit fully."

Elliot's heart raced as the gravity of those words sunk in. To commit meant more than just embracing the music industry; it meant aligning himself with a lifestyle that danced on the edge of morality. The vision of himself as a successful producer began to blur, morphing into an image he hardly recognized—one that thrived in a world of excess and secrecy.

As the night wore on, Elliot felt the tension within him mount. The laughter and flirtation of the partygoers became a cacophony, drowning out his thoughts. He watched as deals were brokered in hushed tones, promises exchanged like currency. It was intoxicating, yet it reeked of deception—a world where loyalty was conditional and betrayal lurked just beneath the surface.

He turned to leave the VIP area, his mind racing with possibilities and fears. Outside, the air felt cooler, a stark contrast to the heated atmosphere within. Elliot inhaled deeply, attempting to clear the fog clouding his judgment. This was his chance to make a name for himself, to leave his mark on the music world, but at what cost? The glittering façade of success began to feel like a gilded cage, and he was the one with the key.

With every step he took, the weight of his decision pressed down on him. Did he want to be part of this elite circle, a player in a game where the stakes were more than just fame and fortune? The allure of exclusivity tugged at him, promising everything he had ever wanted. But as the laughter faded into the background, Elliot could almost hear the faint voice of reason calling him back, reminding him of the integrity he held dear.

Torn between desire and principle, he felt trapped in a liminal space where every choice carried profound consequences. The opportunity of a lifetime dangled before him like a shimmering mirage, but he couldn't shake the feeling that behind every door lay a darkness that could swallow him whole. With his heart racing and mind swirling, Elliot found himself at a crossroads, unsure of which path to take.

Would he step into the alluring abyss of ambition, risking his soul for a fleeting taste of success, or would he retreat, preserving his values in a world that seemed increasingly foreign? As he stood there, contemplating his next move, Elliot knew he faced a decision that could shape the course of his life forever.

Chapter 8: Moral Crossroads

Elliot stepped outside, the crisp night air filling his lungs as he sought clarity amid the chaos swirling in his mind. The events of the evening replayed like a haunting melody, echoing his internal conflict. He had spent years dreaming of this moment—the glitz, the glamour, the possibility of making it big in the music industry. But as he leaned against the cool wall of the venue, the shimmering allure of fame began to feel like a double-edged sword.

The laughter and music faded into the background as Elliot reflected on the dreams that had fueled his journey. In the quiet moments of his life, he had envisioned a career built on authenticity, a pursuit of passion that would not only elevate him but also touch the hearts of others. He imagined himself creating songs that inspired, producing sounds that resonated with the struggles and triumphs of real life. Yet now, standing on the precipice of success, he felt an unsettling dissonance between his aspirations and the world unfolding before him.

As he scrolled through his phone, reviewing the photos from the night, he saw smiles and laughter frozen in time, each snapshot a testament to the fun and excitement he had felt. But beneath the surface lay the nagging questions that began to unravel the thread of his ambition. Was he willing to pay the price for this fame? What sacrifices would he need to make to gain acceptance in this elite circle? The whispers of the night crept into his thoughts, warnings that the world of power and influence came with strings attached.

The dichotomy of his desires left him torn. He recalled the small music venues he once played in, the humble beginnings that had stoked his passion. He remembered the thrill of writing songs that felt true to his experiences, the satisfaction of connecting with an audience that resonated with his words. It had always been about the music, the craft, and the ability to share a piece of himself with the world. But now, surrounded by temptation and the promise of success, he felt that essence slipping away.

As he stood there, he couldn't help but think of the stories he had heard about others who had succumbed to the siren call of fame. He had seen friends change in the pursuit of success, compromising their integrity for fleeting moments of recognition. Was he prepared to walk that same path? The thought churned in his stomach, and for the first time, he felt a chill that had nothing to do with the evening air.

His mind wandered to Victor and the other influential figures he had met that night. They seemed so comfortable in their skin, weaving through the party with an effortless confidence that came from years of navigating this world. Yet, beneath their polished exteriors, he sensed the cracks—fleeting moments of vulnerability that hinted at the heavy toll their choices had taken. He couldn't ignore the darker undertones of their conversations, the subtle hints that loyalty could easily be traded for convenience.

FREAK PARTY

Elliot closed his eyes, trying to silence the noise around him. He envisioned the path ahead: one lined with glittering lights and accolades, but overshadowed by the specter of compromise. In stark contrast, there lay the road less traveled, where authenticity reigned, but the destination remained uncertain. Could he navigate this treacherous terrain without losing himself in the process?

As he grappled with these thoughts, the realization hit him like a bolt of lightning—his journey had always been about more than just personal ambition. It was about creating a legacy, leaving a mark that transcended his individual desires. Could he do that in a world where success often meant sacrificing one's principles? The weight of this moral crossroads pressed heavily upon him.

With a deep breath, Elliot pushed himself off the wall, his heart racing with determination. He needed to confront the reality of his choices, to define what success meant for him. Was it the hollow accolades of an industry rife with deception, or was it the genuine connections he could forge through his art? The questions swirled, but one thing was clear: he stood at a pivotal moment in his life, a choice that would shape his identity and ultimately determine the legacy he would leave behind.

With each step, he felt the resolve within him harden. It was time to choose—fame at any cost, or the pursuit of a dream grounded in integrity. The world ahead was uncertain, but Elliot knew he had to be true to himself, regardless of the path he decided to follow. As the party continued to pulse behind him, he took a moment to reflect on who he wanted to be, and he made a silent promise to himself: no matter what lay ahead, he would not compromise his values for the sake of acceptance.

Elliot leaned against the bar, the remnants of the evening buzzing around him like a distant hum. He had just managed to escape the intensity of the VIP room when a familiar figure caught his eye—Jack, a fellow producer he had met early in the night. Jack's demeanor was different now; his usual charm seemed drained, replaced by a disheveled look that spoke of indulgence and excess.

As Elliot watched Jack laugh too loudly at a joke shared among strangers, a tight knot formed in his stomach. He approached, attempting to engage, but Jack's laughter quickly turned to a forced grin that didn't reach his eyes. It was unsettling, this stark contrast between the two sides of the night—on one hand, the sparkling allure of fame and fortune, and on the other, the vulnerability that lurked just beneath the surface.

"Hey, man," Elliot said, offering a smile that felt increasingly hollow. "You good?"

Jack's eyes flickered with something—was it embarrassment? Fear? "Yeah, just... living it up, you know?" His voice was too loud, tinged with an edge that suggested he was trying hard to convince himself.

Elliot's heart raced as he felt the weight of the choices that lay ahead. This wasn't the Jack he had met hours earlier, brimming with ambition and the sparkle of potential. This was a man unraveling at the seams, caught in the very web of excess that Elliot had started to fear.

"Are you sure? You look a bit—" Elliot began, but Jack cut him off with a wave of his hand, dismissing the concern as if it were a pesky fly.

FREAK PARTY 67

"Come on, it's just a party!" Jack's voice raised another notch, and Elliot could see others start to look their way. It was a dance they all knew too well—pretend everything was fine while teetering on the edge of chaos.

Elliot's instinct told him to step back, to ignore the growing pit in his stomach. But instead, he took a chance, reaching out to his friend. "You don't have to pretend with me, Jack. We can talk about it if you want."

At that moment, the mask slipped. Jack's laughter faded, replaced by a haunting silence. He turned away, and for the first time, Elliot saw the cracks beneath the surface. Tears glimmered in Jack's eyes, his facade collapsing. "I don't even know how it got this far," he whispered, the confession barely audible over the party's roar.

Elliot's heart sank as he saw his friend's anguish. Jack stumbled backward, nearly knocking over a table. "I thought I could handle it, but it's all too much. The drugs, the people, the expectations. I don't even recognize myself anymore."

The admission struck Elliot like a punch to the gut. This was not just a moment of weakness; it was a revelation about the very lifestyle he had been drawn into. The weight of Jack's words hung in the air, heavy with the reality that so many others were grappling with behind the glittering façade.

Elliot reached out, grabbing Jack's arm as he swayed unsteadily. "Let's get out of here. We can find somewhere quiet to talk," he urged, his voice firm yet gentle.

Jack hesitated, fear and relief playing across his features. The struggle within him was palpable, but finally, he nodded, and Elliot led him through the crowd, navigating the sea of bodies that danced obliviously to the turmoil unfolding just beyond the spotlight.

Once outside, the cool air washed over them like a cleansing wave. They found a secluded spot, away from the noise and chaos. Jack leaned against the wall, his breath ragged as he struggled to compose himself. Elliot watched, feeling a mix of sympathy and urgency.

"I don't want to end up like one of those guys," Jack finally said, voice shaking. "I don't want to lose everything I worked for. But I don't know how to stop."

Elliot felt his heart ache for his friend. "You're not alone, Jack. We can figure this out together," he replied, unsure if his words would bring comfort or just more confusion.

As they stood in the shadows, the truth of their situation settled heavily around them. Elliot realized that Jack's breakdown was not just a warning sign for him; it was a mirror reflecting the potential consequences of the choices he was about to make. In that moment, he knew he had to decide who he wanted to be in this world.

The night felt darker, and the future more uncertain. Yet, as he stood there with Jack, Elliot understood that the moral crossroads he faced wasn't just about fame or ambition; it was about choosing authenticity over illusion, real connections over shallow indulgence. And with that understanding came a flicker of hope—a chance to reclaim his dreams before they slipped through his fingers like sand.

FREAK PARTY 69

Elliot stood outside the afterparty venue, the cacophony of laughter and music muffled by the thick walls that shielded the hedonistic chaos within. His heart raced as he contemplated leaving, the choice feeling monumental and terrifying. The weight of his decision pressed down on him, almost suffocating. Jack's words echoed in his mind, a haunting reminder of the price of indulgence—a price he was unwilling to pay. Yet, the thought of walking away sent a shiver of doubt coursing through him.

"Maybe I'm just overreacting," he whispered to himself, glancing back at the door that separated him from the allure of fame and influence. There was still a part of him that craved acceptance from the elite crowd inside. He had come so far, after all—receiving that coveted invitation to The White Party felt like a ticket to a world where dreams could manifest into reality. Yet, the more he stood there, the more he understood that this was a world riddled with shadows.

Elliot's mind flickered with images of the people he had met that night—powerful figures whose eyes sparkled with promises, their smiles hiding secrets. The potential connections he could make were intoxicating, but with each thought of stepping back inside, a wave of unease washed over him. He remembered the hollow laughter, the reckless abandon of the guests who seemed to have lost themselves in the very lifestyle he was now questioning.

Desperation clawed at his insides as he turned to leave. "What if I disappoint them?" he thought, feeling the weight of their expectations. They had welcomed him with open arms, showing him the glitz and glamour of their world. The powerful mogul had shown interest in him, offering a glimpse into what could be a bright future. What would they think if he just vanished? Would they see him as weak, ungrateful for the chance to be part of something larger than himself?

His thoughts spiraled as he pictured their faces—fellow producers, the high-profile guests who had laughed with him, the mogul with his magnetic presence. Each image was tainted with the fear of judgment. He felt like a child caught between wanting to play with the big kids and knowing he would be sent home for breaking the rules. In that moment, Elliot's vision blurred with tears that threatened to spill.

He had spent years climbing the industry ladder, navigating the complexities of music production, and had sacrificed so much along the way. The prospect of being seen as someone who couldn't hack it among the elites felt unbearable. "Maybe I just need to stick it out a little longer," he thought, trying to justify his hesitation. "It's just one night, right?"

Yet, deep down, he knew it was more than just a single evening. It was a pivotal moment—a crossroads that would shape not only his career but his very identity. The enticing whispers of ambition battled against the echoes of his principles. He had come to this party hoping to forge connections, but now, it felt like a trap. Elliot's mind raced as he grappled with the realization that the lines between opportunity and exploitation were dangerously blurred.

"Is this who I want to be?" he asked himself, the question hanging heavy in the air. The answer felt painfully clear. He had always dreamed of being a music producer who created meaningful connections and shared powerful stories, not one

FREAK PARTY

who thrived in the shadows of indulgence. Yet, the fear of backlash—of disappointing those who had taken him under their wings—felt like a weight he couldn't bear.

With a deep breath, Elliot stepped away from the door, the noise fading further behind him. He was making a choice, and it was both liberating and terrifying. The allure of exclusivity and power was still palpable, but he had to honor the man he aspired to be, the dreams he had cultivated long before this night.

As he walked away, the faces of the party faded into the night, replaced by a newfound determination. He realized that the path to success didn't have to be paved with compromises. If he left now, he would reclaim his narrative, choosing integrity over temptation. With each step, Elliot felt lighter, his heart slowly unburdening itself from the weight of false expectations. He may not have known what lay ahead, but he was ready to find out—on his own terms.

Chapter 9: The Fallout

Elliot's decision to extricate himself from the world of hedonistic indulgence was not without consequences. The aftermath of his choice weighed heavily on him, and what had initially seemed like a liberating step toward reclaiming his identity quickly morphed into a haunting struggle against the insidious repercussions of distancing himself from the elite crowd.

In the days following the party, he felt the chill of isolation seep into his life. Initially, he had received supportive texts from friends he had met at the party, assuring him they were looking forward to working together on future projects. But as the days wore on, the frequency of those messages dwindled, replaced by an uncomfortable silence that echoed in his phone. The vibrant connections he had once enjoyed now felt like faint memories, haunting reminders of the camaraderie that had quickly turned into exclusion.

At first, the subtle snubs were easy to dismiss. A delayed response to a casual inquiry here, an unreturned invitation there—it was all part of the ebb and flow of the industry, or so he tried to convince himself. But as he attended industry events and networking parties, the reality became increasingly clear: the insiders had turned their backs on him. The air thickened with tension every time he entered a room, the whispers of his former peers swirling around him like a dark cloud.

The first overt sign of discontent came when Elliot approached a small group of producers he had once considered friends. They were laughing and chatting, their faces lighting up with the warmth of shared stories. But as Elliot stepped closer, their smiles faltered, and an awkward silence ensued. It was as if he had intruded on a private moment. After a few painful seconds, they returned to their conversation, deliberately ignoring him, a stark contrast to the easy camaraderie they had shared before.

Feeling exposed and vulnerable, Elliot retreated to a quieter corner of the venue. The laughter that filled the room now felt like mockery, echoing the doubts swirling in his mind. Was he foolish for standing by his principles? Had he underestimated the depths of loyalty in this cutthroat world? The uncertainty gnawed at him, a relentless reminder that his decision had set him apart from those who thrived in the shadows.

As days turned into weeks, the subtle threats began to surface. A casual comment from a stranger about the dangers of speaking out in the industry felt like a veiled warning. The way insiders looked at him—once warm and inviting—now carried a sharp edge, their gazes lingering with an unsettling intensity. The whispers grew louder, and the gossip spread like wildfire. Stories of Elliot's retreat from the party scene morphed into tales of betrayal, painting him as an outsider who had turned his back on the opportunities he had been given.

Elliot soon found himself at an industry gathering, where the atmosphere was charged with unspoken animosity. He spotted a familiar face across the room—one of the mogul's trusted associates—engaged in a hushed conversation with another insider. Their eyes flickered toward Elliot, and a smirk

FREAK PARTY   75

danced on the lips of the associate. In that moment, Elliot felt the weight of their scrutiny, the invisible strings of the social web tightening around him.

Anxiety bubbled to the surface, and he sensed danger lurking just beyond his periphery. It was a stark reminder that he was no longer part of the privileged circle, a reality that left him feeling vulnerable. Each social snub felt like a calculated move to push him further into the shadows, a reminder that the world he had tried to distance himself from was still watching.

Feeling increasingly trapped, Elliot contemplated reaching out to those he had once considered allies. Perhaps they would still support him, offer some semblance of reassurance amid the turmoil. But as he hesitated, he recalled their glances—cold, calculating, filled with an unspoken understanding that he had stepped out of line.

Days turned into nights filled with sleeplessness, his mind a turbulent sea of worry. The once vibrant dreams of music production were overshadowed by a looming fear that threatened to swallow him whole. The industry he had longed to be a part of now felt like a dangerous game, and he was just one move away from being completely out of the picture.

Caught in this treacherous web, Elliot faced a grim reality: his decision to prioritize integrity over indulgence had come at a high cost. The fallout was real, and he could no longer ignore the fact that his past choices had left him exposed, a pariah in a world that once promised him everything. The question loomed in his mind: was he prepared to fight for his place, or would he be swallowed by the shadows he had tried to escape?

Elliot had always prided himself on his ability to network and cultivate relationships in the music industry, but as he scanned his phone for updates, a sinking feeling settled in the pit of his stomach. What was once a stream of opportunities had turned into a desolate silence. The whispers he had heard about his retreat from the party scene began to morph into something darker—something that threatened to unravel the very fabric of his career.

He had received a call from a producer he had been hoping to work with on an upcoming project. The conversation had started with a friendly tone but quickly shifted when the producer hesitated, carefully choosing his words. "I'm sorry, Elliot. I've heard some things. You know how it is... things get around in this business." The words felt like a punch to the gut, leaving Elliot reeling. He felt the walls closing in as he realized that someone had been spreading damaging rumors about him, sabotaging the very connections he had worked so hard to build.

After hanging up, he paced his apartment, his mind racing. Who could be behind this? The only explanation was that someone within that exclusive circle had taken offense at his decision to withdraw from their lifestyle. He recalled the glares, the whispers, the tension—those subtle signs he had brushed off in the hope that it was merely paranoia. But now, it was clear: someone had decided he was a threat, and they were determined to erase him from the scene.

With every passing moment, the isolation pressed down on him like a heavy weight. He was trapped in a whirlwind of confusion and betrayal. Hadn't he been one of them, sharing laughter and dreams only days ago? The irony of it all gnawed at him. He had chosen integrity, and in return, he was being

FREAK PARTY

punished. The elitist atmosphere that once felt so thrilling now felt like a suffocating prison, its bars crafted from the judgments of those he thought were friends.

Desperation fueled his determination to uncover the truth. Elliot began reaching out to the few contacts he had left—people who still seemed willing to talk to him. Each conversation only deepened his resolve, revealing more about the underbelly of the industry. It was a landscape rife with backstabbing and manipulation, where reputations could be torn down with a single, whispered word. He was a pawn in a game he barely understood, and he needed to figure out who was pulling the strings.

His investigation led him to a small gathering of aspiring producers. They were eager to share the latest gossip, and Elliot took the opportunity to press them for information. One of them mentioned a meeting that had taken place shortly after he pulled away from the party scene, where insiders had gathered to discuss who would be "in" and who would be "out." The implication was clear: Elliot's name had come up, and not in a favorable light. He felt a chill run down his spine as he imagined the discussions that had taken place, the decisions that had been made at his expense.

Fueled by this new information, Elliot dug deeper. He began to piece together the timeline, connecting dots between the various figures who had once welcomed him into their world. His instincts told him that it was not just one person but a collective decision made by those who felt threatened by his sudden withdrawal. The very people he had thought were allies were now the architects of his downfall.

Determined to confront the shadows that loomed over him, Elliot sought out a close acquaintance who had remained neutral amid the chaos. He hoped that perhaps this person could shed light on the situation. When they finally met at a quiet café, Elliot laid bare his fears and suspicions. The acquaintance listened intently, their brow furrowed in concern. "It's a ruthless game, Elliot. You were a rising star, and when you stepped back, it left a gap. They'll fill it with someone else—someone who won't rock the boat."

The words struck a nerve, resonating with the fear that had taken root in Elliot's heart. He realized he had not only lost friendships; he had unwittingly placed himself in the crosshairs of an industry that valued loyalty over integrity. As the conversation deepened, he could feel the weight of uncertainty settle in—a haunting reminder of the precariousness of his situation.

Elliot left the café with a mix of resolve and dread. He could no longer afford to be passive; the shadows were closing in, and he needed to reclaim his narrative. The realization that he was isolated and vulnerable in a world that once held promise was a bitter pill to swallow, but it also ignited a fire within him. He had a choice to make: either succumb to the pressure and let the whispers dictate his fate or fight back, reclaiming his voice and the integrity he so desperately wanted to hold onto.

As he walked through the bustling streets, Elliot felt the determination surge within him. The fallout was real, but so was his resolve to confront it head-on. He would not let the shadows win. It was time to expose the truths lurking beneath the surface, to fight for his place in an industry that had suddenly turned hostile. The journey ahead would be challenging, but he was

FREAK PARTY

prepared to face the storm that lay ahead. He would fight for his career, his dreams, and the life he had envisioned long before the allure of exclusivity had clouded his judgment.

Elliot sat on the edge of his bed, the weight of the world pressing down on him as he stared at the blank wall. His mind raced with the events of the past few weeks, each moment replaying like a broken record. The parties, the whispers, the sudden shift in the attitude of those he once considered friends—it all converged into a storm of uncertainty. He was stuck between a rock and a hard place, and the tension was suffocating.

Fearing for his safety, he felt the urgency of his situation sharpen. The subtle threats had grown bolder, turning from veiled warnings into explicit implications that made his skin crawl. He had received anonymous messages hinting that there were consequences for his decisions to pull away from their world. "You don't want to know what happens to those who think they can just walk away," one had read. The anonymity only fueled his paranoia, making him question who was watching him, who might be lurking in the shadows, waiting for him to slip up.

As he paced his small apartment, the idea of exposing the truth behind the parties flickered in his mind. The allure of revealing the hedonistic, corrupt underbelly of the mogul's elite gatherings felt like a siren's call, promising a release from his turmoil. Yet, the thought also sent chills down his spine. Would it ruin his career? Would it be worth the fallout that could come from shaking the very foundation of an industry that thrived on secrecy and exclusivity? The risk was immense, and the stakes higher than he ever imagined.

Elliot grappled with the notion that bringing the truth to light could either save him or destroy him. He recalled the desperation in the eyes of his friend who had broken down at the party, a stark reminder of the price people paid to fit into this lavish lifestyle. Those memories mingled with his anger towards the corrupt practices that surrounded him, igniting a fierce sense of responsibility within him. If he could expose the darkness that lurked behind the glitz, could he also protect others from falling prey to its charms?

He envisioned the aftermath of such revelations: media scrutiny, potential legal battles, and the irrevocable loss of the connections he had fought so hard to build. The thought of facing those powerful figures, the mogul among them, filled him with dread. They had the means to crush someone like him—a mere young producer in a world of titans. He could imagine their disdain, their fury at being outed, and the lengths they might go to protect their empire.

Yet, another voice within him whispered of the possibility of change. Perhaps the truth could catalyze a shift in the industry, forcing it to confront its demons. He thought about other aspiring producers who might be lured into the same trap he had narrowly escaped. If he remained silent, what message would that send? Was he willing to sacrifice his principles for the sake of his career? He had already experienced firsthand the consequences of that kind of compromise.

As the evening darkened, Elliot found himself at a moral crossroads. The phone in his pocket buzzed with notifications, but he ignored it, lost in his thoughts. He had to make a decision: would he step into the light and reveal what he knew, or would he retreat into the shadows, preserving his safety but sacrificing his integrity?

The prospect of taking a stand thrilled and terrified him in equal measure. He could be the voice for those who felt voiceless, the beacon that guided others away from the allure of a toxic lifestyle. But could he bear the potential repercussions, both personal and professional? His heart raced as he weighed the consequences against the potential impact of his actions. The idea of being a whistleblower was daunting, yet the idea of remaining complicit in the deception felt like a betrayal of everything he had once aspired to be.

He sat down at his desk, pulled out a blank notebook, and began jotting down his thoughts. Clarity emerged as he wrote, the pen gliding over the pages as he poured his heart out. Each word was a step closer to understanding what he truly wanted—what he was willing to fight for.

In that moment of solitude, Elliot realized he had to reclaim his narrative. Whether he chose to expose the truth or find another path, he needed to make a choice that aligned with his values. The fallout was real, but so was his chance to redefine his future, and he refused to let fear dictate his decisions any longer. The music industry might be a treacherous place, but it was his life, and he was determined to navigate it on his own terms.

Chapter 10: The Escape

Elliot sat in the dim light of his apartment, surrounded by a haze of uncertainty. The walls felt closer than ever, each echoing the whispers of the industry he yearned to escape. Days of swirling tension had culminated in this moment, where clarity began to break through the fog. His heart raced with the thought of leaving the high-stakes world behind, a realm filled with deception and moral decay. He knew he had to act before the weight of his choices crushed him completely.

Sifting through the clutter on his desk, he pulled out a sheet of paper, its surface marred by hasty notes and crossed-out ideas. He had been brainstorming ways to dismantle the connections that tethered him to the mogul's shadow. Each name listed represented a network of influence, a dangerous web spun from ambition and betrayal. But as he traced the ink with his finger, he felt the familiar pang of doubt. Could he truly cut these ties without facing dire consequences?

Elliot knew the industry was not forgiving, especially for someone who dared to reject its allure. Yet the thought of continuing on this path felt like a betrayal to everything he once stood for. He envisioned the day he stepped into this world—filled with hope and the desire to create art that mattered. Now, his dreams lay tarnished, obscured by the glimmering facade of wealth and excess. He took a deep breath, steeling himself against the memories of that initial excitement.

His plan began to take shape as he recalled the advice of a mentor who had once said, "Integrity is the foundation of your career." He had let that foundation crumble in pursuit of acceptance, but now he was determined to rebuild it. Elliot's first step would be to sever his ties with the mogul. This would be no easy feat; the mogul was known for his reach, his influence extending into every corner of the industry.

Elliot decided he needed to create a diversion. The mogul's parties had always been extravagant, filled with distractions that kept attendees enthralled. If Elliot could stage a faux scandal, something that would draw attention away from him, he could make his exit under the radar. His mind raced with ideas—could he leak a rumor? Perhaps a controversy about an upcoming project? Something that would divert the mogul's gaze away from him, even if only temporarily.

With the seed of an idea planted, Elliot began to formulate a plan. He would approach a journalist he had crossed paths with at one of the parties. The journalist had always been interested in the darker side of the industry, and perhaps he would be willing to run a story about the mogul's questionable practices. Elliot just needed to provide the right amount of bait—a hint of scandal that would entice the journalist without implicating himself too closely.

As he crafted his narrative, Elliot felt a surge of adrenaline coursing through him. For the first time in a long while, he felt a flicker of hope. He could reclaim his integrity without abandoning the art he loved. He envisioned a life free from the chains of manipulation, a life where he could create without compromise.

FREAK PARTY 85

But with every action, there were risks. Elliot knew he had to tread carefully, keeping his plans close to his chest. The mogul had eyes everywhere, and he wouldn't hesitate to crush anyone who dared to undermine his empire. Yet the very thought of continuing down this dark path was more terrifying than any threat the mogul could pose.

Elliot's resolve strengthened. He jotted down notes for the story he would present to the journalist, ensuring that every detail was meticulously crafted. He imagined himself finally free—no longer tethered to a world that had lost its luster. In that moment of clarity, he vowed to reclaim his narrative and his life, not allowing anyone to dictate his worth.

The plan was set in motion, but he knew it would take every ounce of courage he had to see it through. With a final glance at the notes before him, he felt the weight of the world begin to lift. It was time to act, to reclaim his destiny before the mogul could tighten his grip once more.

The city's skyline glimmered under the night sky, but Elliot found no beauty in the lights that once inspired him. Instead, he felt the weight of secrecy pressing against him, a constant reminder of the risks he was taking. After spending hours meticulously planning his departure from the mogul's world, he realized he wouldn't be able to do it alone. He needed help—a trusted ally who understood the stakes.

His mind raced to Sarah, an old friend from his early days in the industry. They had bonded over shared dreams of success and authenticity, but as Elliot ascended into the high-stakes world of the mogul, their paths diverged. Sarah had stepped back, unwilling to compromise her values in the face of rampant ambition. But now, she might be the very person he needed to navigate this dangerous terrain.

Elliot hesitated as he typed her name into his phone. Would she even be willing to help him after all this time? He was about to reach out when his phone buzzed. It was a text from her: *"Hey, thinking of you. How are things?"*

With a surge of adrenaline, he responded, explaining his predicament and his plan to escape the mogul's grasp. He kept it brief, knowing that the less detail he provided, the better. To his surprise, her response came quickly: *"Meet me at our old café. We need to talk."*

The familiar warmth of the café brought back a flood of memories as Elliot arrived. It was a small, intimate spot, their sanctuary during more innocent times when dreams felt within reach. Sarah was already seated, her eyes scanning the room with a mix of caution and determination.

"Elliot," she said, her voice steady but filled with concern as he sat down. "I didn't expect to see you here again. What's going on?"

He took a deep breath, the weight of his choices crashing down on him as he laid out the details of his escape plan. He spoke of the mogul's influence, the power he wielded, and how Elliot could no longer bear the weight of the secrets that surrounded him. Sarah listened intently, her brow furrowing as he described the underbelly of the parties and the pressure to conform.

"Are you sure you want to do this?" she asked, her voice softening. "It's not just about leaving; it's about the consequences."

FREAK PARTY 87

Elliot nodded, the reality settling deep within him. "I've thought it through. I can't continue living like this. But I need your help to make it happen."

After a moment of silence, Sarah leaned closer, her eyes filled with resolve. "I know people who can help. But we have to be careful. If the mogul gets wind of this—"

"I know," he interrupted, his voice firm. "That's why I'm counting on you. I trust you."

With that, they began to formulate a plan. Sarah had connections that could provide Elliot with a safe passage out of the city, away from the industry that had nearly consumed him. They mapped out a route that would keep him off the mogul's radar.

"Here's the deal," Sarah said, her tone shifting to serious. "You'll need to lay low for a while. I'll help you with contacts who can get you out, but you have to promise me you won't look back."

Elliot felt a mix of gratitude and fear. This was it—the point of no return. He nodded, his resolve crystallizing. "I promise."

As they finalized the details, Elliot felt a weight lift off his shoulders. He realized that the support of a true friend made all the difference. This wasn't just about escaping; it was about reclaiming his identity, free from the shadows that had loomed over him for so long.

Later that night, as Elliot prepared to leave, he glanced around the apartment that had become a cage. He thought of his dreams—now tinged with the reality of what he'd faced. But with Sarah's help, he was ready to step into the unknown.

He gathered his belongings, the significance of each item hitting him hard. They were remnants of a life he was determined to leave behind. As he walked out the door for the last time, he felt a surge of hope mixed with apprehension. With Sarah by his side, he was no longer just fleeing; he was choosing to forge a new path, one that would allow him to reclaim his integrity and his passion for music. The escape had begun, and for the first time in a long while, Elliot felt alive.

As Elliot walked through the dimly lit streets, the cool night air wrapped around him like a comforting embrace, a stark contrast to the suffocating atmosphere of the parties he had left behind. Each step away from the life he had known felt heavy with the weight of reflection. He could almost hear the echoes of laughter and the pulsating beats of music fading into the distance, replaced by the quiet murmur of his thoughts.

He thought about the cost of fame—what it had meant to him, what he had sacrificed in the pursuit of success. The allure of glittering parties, the promise of connections, and the tantalizing whispers of future greatness had once blinded him. But now, all he could see were the shadows cast by his ambition. He had been so eager to rise that he had failed to notice how close he had come to losing himself entirely.

Fame, he realized, came with strings attached. The industry thrived on secrets, and those secrets had a way of festering, threatening to consume anyone who dared to get too close. Elliot had seen the toll it took on his peers—the desperation behind their smiles, the hollow eyes of those who had indulged too deeply in the lifestyle. He thought of Sarah's warnings, the countless times she had expressed her concerns about the dangers lurking beneath the surface of their shared dreams.

FREAK PARTY 89

As he continued to walk, a wave of clarity washed over him. He had spent so much time chasing validation, seeking approval from those who barely knew him. The validation he craved came with compromises that gnawed at his conscience. He thought about the young artists he had hoped to support, their potential overshadowed by the whims of powerful moguls. He had wanted to be a voice for the unheard, yet he found himself trapped in a system that thrived on exploitation and deception.

Now, standing at this crossroads, he understood the importance of pursuing a new path—one defined by his own terms. He had to let go of the notion that success was synonymous with wealth and influence. True success, he decided, lay in authenticity, in the courage to stand up for what he believed in. The music industry could be a vehicle for creativity and connection, but only if he approached it with integrity.

His resolve strengthened with each thought. He envisioned a future where he could help artists navigate the complexities of the industry without compromising their values. He wanted to create a space where talent could flourish, free from the chains of greed and manipulation. Elliot longed for a life that didn't revolve around the glitz and glamour but rather focused on genuine connection and artistic expression.

As the moon hung high in the sky, Elliot took a deep breath, feeling lighter as he left the past behind. He was determined to carve out a new identity for himself—one that was not tied to the shadows of his former life. With every step, he felt the chains of secrecy and regret breaking away, freeing him to rediscover his passion for music.

He resolved to embrace vulnerability, understanding that it was okay to be imperfect. The scars of his past would serve as reminders of the lessons learned and the strength he had gained. With renewed purpose, he vowed to share his story with others who might feel lost in the same tumultuous sea of ambition.

Tonight marked the beginning of his journey toward reclaiming his narrative, of shining a light on the truths he had once hidden from. He would no longer be a pawn in a game that prioritized power over principle. Instead, Elliot would be an advocate for change, a champion of authenticity in an industry rife with shadows.

As he stepped forward into the night, Elliot felt a sense of peace settle within him. The world was vast and uncertain, but for the first time in a long while, he felt hopeful. The dark side of the industry may have tried to ensnare him, but he had found the strength to break free. The future was unwritten, and he was ready to embrace it on his own terms.

Also by Aiden Rivers

Christmas Thriller
Christmas Eve Revenge
Christmas Lights
The Silent Night Curse

Freak Party
Freak Party
Freak Party: Shadows of Fame

Standalone
Crimes of Passion: The Silence Beneath
Echoes of Obsession
Island of Hearts
The Mirror's Edge
The Shadow Mind
Beyond the Goal: A Love Unwritten
Gay Short Stories
Hearts in the Outfield

Milton Keynes UK
Ingram Content Group UK Ltd.
UKHW041822131124
451149UK00001B/27